Space Murder

.

NL Haverstock

DEDICATION

To Becca Syme.
Thank you for being a great friend and awesome coach.

CONTENTS

For everything there is a season...

Once the star student of her training class, Captain Liz
Laika is now an outcast, a casualty of family scandal. Now
stuck in the worst post in the Fleet, she should keep her
head down. But when a Cerulean passenger is found
decapitated, and Liz is framed for the murder, she has no
choice but to fight for her life. No easy feat when she's
facing kidnapping, ship-eating whales, horse-sized spiders
and corrupt fleet officers with personal vendettas. And in
the middle of the intergalactic murder drama, her ex-fiancé
reappears. Captain Liz needs to clear her name--and fast.

CHAPTER ONE

"Undocking, Liz," my navigation officer said.

The engines revved up, and we slowly backed away from our fueling bay. I should reprimand Raph. Protocol dictated that he request verbal confirmation from me before undocking, and he definitely should have used my title and family name, but I let it go.

There was a time in my life when I would have been horrified by breaking the rules, but that was a long time ago. And what had the rules ever done for me? I let out a sigh when Raph shot me a smirk and set in the navigation coordinates without my approval.

He was a few standardized years younger than I was, but because of his hard-partying lifestyle, he sometimes looked a decade older. He was a rebel, stubborn, and enjoyed getting under my skin.

He was also the reason we were refilling and back on route instead of docked until morning. The secondary team who took over in our off hours was only allowed to continue in the direction we set at the end of shift. They would have docked us until the new shift started at oh nine hundred hours. But when Raph felt the deceleration, he had come to my room to wake me and set a new course.

His action would have us arriving eight hours ahead of schedule and earn the entire crew another delivery bonus.

In the two years since I had taken the helm, we had done this refill seventy times. Despite being the largest ship in the fleet, ours had the smallest fuel supply. Apparently, one of my predecessors had reconfigured our fuel setup to fit more cargo.

I stared out at the Nighthorse galaxy through the thick window that dominated the front wall of the navigation room. The fueling station was at a crossroads where exploration ships headed out. The unexplored galaxy was why I had been training for twenty years. I was supposed to captain a ship that took scientists out to investigate it, perhaps to be the first human to set foot on the next planet to terraform, possibly even, despite all reports so far, to encounter new life.

I sighed and wondered for the millionth time if I was still young enough to quit the fleet to be a trophy wife back on Earth, but I knew I didn't have the temperament to stroke anyone's ego. I was a ship's captain through and through. Delivering mail, supplies, and occasional humans or aliens between two planets wasn't the worst assignment in the entire galaxy. There had to be something worse. I didn't know of anything, but it just had to exist.

The engines ground and clicked as they attempted to move the massive ship to traveling speed. It sounded like someone had thrown an entire silverware set into a massive garbage disposal. The first time I had heard it, I insisted on returning to dock and having the ship checked. The mechanic said there was nothing *technically* wrong with the ship. It had been decommissioned a few decades earlier and recommissioned just for me.

Lucky me.

I had put in a ticket for upgrades, and it was returned four minutes later—from the fleet president to me, personally. *Denied.* It was clear in that moment that even though they had given me a ship, they had no desire to give me help. That was the first and last time I had communicated with the administration. I would never give them the pleasure of denying a request ever again.

The first few weeks had been bumpy, especially with Raph. He had been defiant and basically looking to pick a fight with me, which didn't make sense since he was one report from a dishonorable discharge.

After weeks of grinding my teeth and being professional, I had dragged him into my office. I had been ready to chew him out, but I didn't have enough energy. All my frustration came out in the form of an ultimatum. If he wanted to stay, he had to be professional and get a better attitude while on duty, plus he could never do anything to endanger the ship or anyone on board. That was it. That was all I asked. The choice to stay or leave was his.

He did not kiss my feet in gratitude, but he did stop picking fights. From the gossip I overheard when picking up my meals in the mess hall, he was extremely well-liked by the crew, and he was more focused during work hours. I didn't know how he did it, but our trip, which had been scheduled for twelve days, became ten days. So I let the protocol breaks slide, and I looked the other way when he broke the rules, as long as his transgressions didn't hurt anyone. I would have been a terrible parent.

And when I had answered my door earlier in a set of pink flannel pajamas covered in rainbow unicorns, my hair disheveled and my body drenched in a thin layer of sweat from constant nightmares, he had ignored my appearance. In return, I had ignored his tequila breath. But when I suggested we grab some coffee to help us wake up, he'd listened to me and taken the cue to take a sober-up shot, a nauseating but effective way to counteract alcohol or anything else he had in his system.

My ship was a collection of poor repairs and misfit crew members. But it ran. And we often received delivery bonuses because of the extra cargo space and the speed of the old box of bolts. That made the crew happy. Happy crew, happy life. I might as well earn as much as I could before retirement in forty years. Then maybe I could lie on a beach and forget I was a could-have-been.

A small explorer vessel, an MCXT100, came into view, and my stomach twisted with jealousy. They were the newest class of ships designed for the Nighthorse galaxy exploration. I had read that training was done and the first batch would be sent out this month. That was why I didn't keep up on fleet news. It was a knife in the gut.

A pinging noise filled the room.

"Liz, they're calling. What could they want?" Raph turned to me with a raised eyebrow.

I ran a hand through my fuzzy brown hair, trying to get it all faced in the same direction. "Put them through."

An image popped up on one side of the window, a woman my age with silky black hair pulled back into a slick bun, modest but attractive makeup, and a perfectly pressed uniform. She quickly fell into a speech. "Greetings! This is Captain Jane Luke of the MCXT100 The Destiny. Oh my gosh, is that *Goldie?*"

Horror then nausea rose in my throat. I corrected her. "Captain Elizabeth Laika."

"Silly me. Of course you won't go by Goldie. You aren't the Golden child anymore. And you certainly don't want to be called Lying Liz." Jane attempted to look concerned, but her eyes flashed with glee. "Why are you still in your pajamas? Are you okay?"

Of all the captains of all the starships in the universe, it had to be her. I swallowed down my nausea and took a deep, calming breath. "We are on reverse hours." I clenched my hands into fists with a rage I didn't think I was capable of feeling anymore.

Delight that she didn't even attempt to contain crossed her face. "Oh, that's right. You're doing those little delivery runs. Just thankful for a job, am I right? Well, we are heading—"

"Captain Luke," I said abruptly. "According to protocol 14.5.678b *and* e, you need to state your reason for communication. Otherwise, I will be forced to end transmission." She had always struggled to remember the codes. I felt petty for rubbing it in, but I couldn't help myself.

A sour look crossed her face, and the crew member behind her smirked. Apparently, she was still annoying people.

"I request that since your craft has been undocked for five minutes, you start moving. We needed to be refuel." In her frustration, her accent slipped, and her conjugation went awry. Universal Language was the fleet-required communication form. Her mastery of it had been suspect in college, and apparently, she hadn't put in the time to improve.

"We are moving."

Genuine confusion crossed her face. "You're *not* moving. Maybe drifting a bit. Do you need one of our navigators to help your Claran navigator?"

Raph grumbled under his breath. "I could navigate circles around anyone in this whole—"

I spoke over him, secure in the knowledge that the comm was calibrated not to pick up on his mutterings. "We are a class-fifteen vessel. This is how quickly it accelerates. When we are free, you will be able to fuel. May your journey be safe."

I ended the communication, watching carefully that the light went from green to red to indicate the line was closed. "Sure would be a shame if Captain Jane was eaten by giant space bugs."

Raph snorted. "Why, Cap, I believe that was unbecoming of a high-ranking officer, but it was well deserved. But it would break my heart to see a beautiful ship like that hurt."

I struggled to look away from the ship. With her smooth planes and curved lines, she was truly the most beautiful thing I had ever seen in my life. I could only grunt in agreement.

"Why is she so pissed at you? You sleep with her husband?"

"We were in flight school together."

He rubbed his chin. "She looks really familiar."

I debated how to answer. I could pretend not to know, but then he would look it up himself, and I would look like a coward. "She was one of the key witnesses at my trial. Let's finish up and get out of here."

He nodded. "If you want, I could just bump into them a little."

I chuckled at the idea but shook my head. I double-checked and confirmed our bearings while the engines got us up to speed and slowly moved us from the docking station toward our delivery point. Once we slipped into intraspace, the rest of the trip should be pretty standard, and in five days, we would deliver our cargo and five passengers before starting the return trip.

When the door opened, I didn't turn, but Chloe's heavy breathing made me look up. I noticed her already pale complexion was ashy white, and there were green blotches all over her outfit.

"A passenger is dead!"

CHAPTER TWO

Chloe looked between us for guidance, but Raph and I were both stunned into silence. I was trying to remember the latest passenger list. We usually had a few humanoids or aliens that were willing to take the slow ship to their destination in exchange for rock-bottom prices.

In addition to Chloe's duties preparing the food for the crew and passengers, she also acted as a nurse, a fact I suddenly remembered. "Were they sick? Was it an accident?"

"I don't know." She wrung her hands as her eyes darted around the room. Her breathing was shallow and rapid.

I wondered if medical assistance could save them. "Show me where they are. Raph, finish up here."

Chloe turned and darted out into the hallway, taking the corner like a hyperbike on an obstacle course. I fell into step behind her only to discover Raph at my side.

I tried to tell him to go back and follow my orders, but one syllable in, I knew I didn't have the cardiovascular fitness to run flat out and talk. The ship was large, and the passenger rooms were quite a distance away from us. There were transport pods, but like everything else on the ship, they were old and unreliable. During our first trip, the cleaning staff had become trapped in one and couldn't be removed until we docked. It wasn't surprising that they disembarked and ran away screaming.

Instead of attempting to give a command while huffing and puffing, I balled up my fists and pushed hard to get ahead of him, my fuzzy bunny slippers slapping on the floor of the corridor. The floor beneath us bounced slightly, and there was a creaking with each stride that was amplified and echoed in the hallway.

Raph's long limbs, natural athletic build, and extracurricular activities meant he easily matched my speed. The three of us fell into an easy rhythm, and it suddenly felt good to stretch my legs. A few heads poked out into the hallway then disappeared, which was good because any attempt to identify them would have led to tangled legs and feet.

For a ship this size, the crew was very small, only around two dozen, and of those, most cycled in and out every few months as they either retired, changed jobs, or moved on to better ships. Our ship was a short-term stop on others' journeys of life. In fact, Raph and Chloe were two of the three crew members that had been with me since I had taken control of the ship.

Chloe slowed a little, the gills beneath her ears heaving and flapping to grab any extra oxygen from the air. Her pale complexion was turning pinky orange from the exertion.

On her home planet, humans had adapted to live half their life underwater, catching fish in the cold deep. She didn't handle the heat all that well, and the rich diet on board had curved out her figure significantly. As she ran, she grunted and heaved loudly, which thankfully covered up my own wheezing.

Raph's dark complexion was indicative of his origin on the incredibly bright planet of Clara, and combined with his expressive eyes and easy smile, he was the epitome of conventionally handsome. The females on the ship enthusiastically agreed.

His height and long limbs and fingers were perfect for the complex movements required to pilot a high-end ship with its extensive control panel. It was a shame that since our ship moved slower than a terrestrial snail, he was seldom able to apply his skills to the fullest.

The fleet had the official stance that humans had left Earth thousands of years ago and populated other planets then used science to rapidly evolve. But that viewpoint was not held by everyone. Many planets had created their own origin stories, and who was I to judge? Whatever had happened, it'd been a long time ago, and contact had only been made again within the past few centuries. On Earth, a lot of our official records had been destroyed, along with some of the science required to travel the stars, in a dozen or so unfortunate world wars that set Earth technology back over and over again.

All that was history. We were on the verge of a new age of discovery. At least some people were. I was just trying to keep my heart from exploding as I trotted down three flights of stairs, but I would rather die than admit I wanted to slow down.

Raph earned my eternal hatred as we hit the bottom flight. "This is great. You both should come jogging with me more often."

I turned to say something to him, even if it killed me, when the nose of my right bunny slipper caught on something, and I was flung to the floor at great speed. Even with slightly less than Earth's gravity, I hit the floor of the hallway hard enough to rattle my teeth, and the stitch in my side burned with a tearing sensation that made me grit my teeth as I faced the floor.

"Captain Laika, are you okay?" Chloe leaned over me, her shirt falling forward enough to give me an eyeful. Her skin was iridescent from the layer of sweat, pinks, oranges, and blues seeming to dance across her skin.

As I twisted around to answer her, pain shot through me.

Raph let out a long whistle. "It looks like you've been shivved. Don't move."

If I looked down, I might not be able to hold it together. I held his gaze instead. "I have never been good with blood," I gritted out, "especially my own."

"Then don't look down, Cap. There's blood every— ouch! What was that for?" He spun around to glare at Chloe.

She put her hands on her hips. "Your bedside manner is awful. The captain is bleeding out! And you're *not* making it any better."

A third face joined them, angular, pointed, and most notably, covered in green scales. Horton stood on two legs most of the time, and he had two arms, but that was where the human similarities ended. His features and anatomy were reptilian, including a short thick tail that fell to his hocks. He occasionally wore a shirt but, at the moment, was present in all his scaly glory. I squeezed my eyes shut.

"That was quite a tumble, Capt'n. I swear I could hear y'all banging away for the last two minutes. I was worried the entire da'gum ship was gonna crumble. Lift up your little pink unicorns and let us see how bad it is."

I pulled up my shirt, feeling the hot, sticky blood spreading up my rib cage as I moved the fabric then a thick trickle running down my side and onto the metal below me. After an eternity of poking and prodding, Horton disappeared.

My eyes popped open in time to see Chloe pull out her work unit and kneel over me to get readings. Her work unit was a small hand-sized rectangular device as thick as two fingers. Programs and sensors were installed to help us do our jobs, though I knew that most of us had games and other distractions on them to help pass the time. Since she acted as on-board nurse, she had all the medical software installed.

"Just a bad cut," she said. "No internal damage, but you sure bleed a lot. We should probably run a panel soon."

Horton returned. He was radiating heat as was the open door behind him that led to the engine room. Because of his biology, he enjoyed temperatures that would kill most living creatures.

Between gasps, I addressed him while the three of them looked at my wound. "You're running the engine too hot," I said.

He waved a four-taloned hand in my direction. "It's good for Eugene to run hotter at night. We waste a lot of energy keeping it at the freezing-cold temperatures the fleet recommends."

That was probably part of the reason that we were making such good time on our delivery trips. But I was a bit worried that I was hallucinating. "Eugene?" I choked out.

"Oh! It's just what I call the engine. Nothing more." He laughed nervously. "Now hold very still. The cut isn't too bad, but you'll bleed like a stuck ash-pig if we leave it like this."

Chloe leaned over me, gesturing wildly. "No, I don't think—"

Whether she stopped talking or I stopped hearing her, I was unsure because my own screaming blocked everything out. A scalding heat burned into my side with an intensity that made me feel like my chest cavity was going to explode. My screaming faded as I ran out of air in my lungs, but I continued to make odd squeaking noises. I realized I was jerking my body around like a puppet whose strings were attached to a puppy, but Chloe and Raph were trying to hold me down with their weight on my shoulders and arms.

Black spots were dancing in front of my eyes, and ten thousand years passed before the raging pain stopped, though shock spasms still bounced around my body.

Horton stood up, and his forked tongue darted out to lick each of his eyeballs. "There. Good as new. If you need me, just holler." When he pulled the door shut behind him, the sudden lack of heat was unsettling.

I drew in a deep, shuddering breath.

Chloe stood up and faced Raph. "How could you let him do that? You should have stopped him!"

"Me?" He stood to face her. "I'm not in charge of medical stuff. He seemed to know what he was doing."

"He didn't wash up or give pain meds or anything."

I interrupted them with a long gurgling attempt at speech. "Errrr." I took another shuddering breath. "What?"

Chloe learned over me, her coloring more green than pink, and put on her cheeriest voice. "No worries about your little cut. Horton… took care of it."

The pain radiating across my body was no longer all-consuming but rather focused in my midsection. I weakly raised a hand, and they pulled me to a seated position. "What smells like bacon?"

Raph swallowed. "That's you."

"I was scared you would say that. Can you help me stand?" Once I was on my feet, I finally looked down before jerking my head up again. I had seen enough blood on my torn pajamas and on the floor next to the rugged bit of jagged metal sticking up to know that I wasn't in any shape to look at my side just yet. "What did he cauterize the wound with?"

Raph offered me a steadying arm. "He stuck one of those long nails on his hands through the engine venting and heated it up. That was the most hardcore thing I have ever seen. Cap, you want me to walk you back?"

I took a step and found I could move reasonably well. I pulled away from him. "I think I can make it." The pain was ebbing, and I still had a situation to deal with. "Chloe, which room is it? And someone make sure that floor is fixed."

Chloe started walking much slower than before. "You got it," she said, bursting into a relieved smile. "And the room is right up here. I mean, maybe I was wrong and the guy is okay."

I walked next to her, holding my side and trying not to breathe. "Wrong? I thought you said he was dead?"

"I don't know a lot about Ceruleans. Any chance they don't need their heads?"

Raph let out a whistle.

I shook my head slightly. "No such luck."

She went to the door and pressed the button. The door opened as smoothly as it could, catching and stuttering while letting out a high-pitched screech.

I looked into the room. A male form, slightly blue, lay on the bed in a pool of congealed greenish-black liquid. I turned to the right, and on the single table was the head, the tongue protruding and the eyes staring blankly, surrounded by a puddle of green blood that had dripped onto the floor.

I opened my mouth to say something, but the world swirled around me and went black.

CHAPTER THREE

Four faces floated over me until I was able to focus, then there were just Raph and Chloe looking down on me. I had a strong sense of déjà vu, though I didn't know why or why I was lying down or what we were doing.

"You okay, Cap?" Raph asked.

The genuine concern in his eyes freaked me out more than anything else. "I'm fine. Fine, fine, fine." I tried to sit up, but a shooting pain from rib cage to hip bone stopped me, and I flopped back down. "Fine," I choked out.

Slowly, the memories flitted back to me. First, I remembered the fall and the barbecue job Horton had done on me, which made my stomach roll with nausea. Then I recalled the body on the bed and the head on the table. I swooned a little and swallowed hard to push it away. I was thankful to already be lying down. "Sorry," I said tightly. "It must have been the blood loss."

Raph helped me to my feet and propped me against a wall. "Sure. Right. Of course, Cap. I have some bad news. When you fainted, you landed in a big pool of dead-guy blood."

Chloe sniffed. "Don't be crude. He was a person... or something."

"You want me to pass out like she did?" Raph pointed at me.

I pushed myself upright and raised my hand. "Enough. I need to call the administration about this."

"Whoa. No way. I say we just close the door and pretend we didn't see a thing."

That was not possible, but it did raise a question. "Chloe, why did you go in the room to begin with?"

She blushed a delicate orangey-pink color, and her gills flapped nervously. "I got a note with a hundred standard currency units attached, asking for a dozen of those green cookies I made. It instructed me to bring them in and put them on the table and said I would get another hundred. Imagine if I hadn't. No one would have known."

Raph shook his head. "You were set up."

Her eyes were wide. "Someone did it on purpose?"

"Dear, sweet, dumb Chloe."

She sucked in a breath.

I held up a hand to cut them both off. Chloe had broken a lot of rules, but Raph wasn't far behind. I, on the other hand, was going to play it straight. "Clearly, it was murder, and the sooner we get someone out here, the better."

Under his breath, Raph muttered, "Dear, sweet, dumb Cap."

"Enough." I debated going back to the navigation room to use the large communications screen, but a quick look down showed my rainbow unicorns swimming through green alien blood and leftover gore from my accident, not to mention the large tear that exposed my blood-covered midsection. I patted my pockets, but my work unit was still charging in my room. That left the comm screen in the room. It would only show my face, and I could justify its use as an emergency.

I took a breath and turned to face my crew. "I know it feels like we had a little shared moment, but I am still the captain, and this is my decision. Speaking of which, maybe it's time we tightened up protocol around here." I tried to look stern and captainly.

Chloe pursed her lips and held back a giggle.

Raph nodded. "Sure thing, Captain Laika."

I was pretty sure his reply was more about pity than genuine compliance.

I walked into the room and adjusted the camera so the body on the bed wasn't obvious, then I typed in my credentials and signaled fleet headquarters. I reached a bored-looking receptionist who confirmed that I was who I said I was then took down my request.

"A passenger has been killed, and all signs indicate it was a homicide. Please send a police unit to investigate."

She typed away, not even a flicker of concern crossing her face as she ran through a list of questions that I answered as best I could. Then she sent a locked sequence for us to use to seal the room. "Expect an official reply within four hours and a unit to appear within twenty-four hours," she said in a bored voice. "Until then, you can hold course but no docking. Any questions?"

"No," I said shortly. After terminating the call, I stepped into the hallway and typed the locking sequence into the pad. "Let's head back to bed. I probably won't hear anything for a—" I stopped when a ding rang on both Chloe's and Raph's work units.

Raph pulled his out. "Police unit expected in four hours. Cap, that's not a good sign."

A shiver of panic ran up my spine. "They probably just already had someone in the area. But we better try to get cleaned up and rested before they arrive. It will be a long day."

***

Realistically, having the police unit arrive in four hours was a good thing. They would show up while most of the crew and passengers were still asleep. I set up a lock alarm, which required that everyone stay in their rooms. Most occupants would assume it was because of debris that could cause turbulence, except the murderer of course, who could guess at the real reason.

I would hand off the whole situation to the police and focus on piloting the ship. That should have been a good thing, but I couldn't shake a feeling of dread. The response from headquarters had come within a minute, almost as if someone was waiting for the call, waiting to catch me screwing up. I tried to tell myself it was just paranoia, but the sensation settled into the back of my head, and I found myself jumping at every sound.

Rather than sit and worry, I disposed of my torn and bloody pajamas and slippers and showered. Finally, I looked at my midsection and the hideous purple-and-red tear that went from my ribs to practically my hipbone. I was still a little lightheaded. I was careful in the shower, and I ached all over, but I had to give Horton credit. The wound was effectively sealed.

I lay down to nap, though I was sure that I would toss and turn. Instead, I slipped into fitful sleep that offered no real rest. I had dreams that I was being chased by something or someone through endless hallways and all the doors were locked. I was getting closer and closer to the engine room as the temperature rose, but every time I tried to turn back, the footsteps got closer. Finally, I woke with a start, gasping for air as my alarm went off.

I got off the bed very carefully, splashed water on my face, and dressed. At the last second, I put on some light makeup, something I hadn't done since my first few weeks of command. I didn't do it out of a sense of vanity but as a distraction from the dark smudges under my eyes and in the vain hope I would appear professional.

I found Raph waiting near the docking hatch. He'd cleaned up and put on a fresh uniform.

"You are supposed to stay in your room."

He avoided my eyes. "I couldn't let you face them alone. I don't trust this whole situation. Something feels off about it. Plus one of them could be a hot lady. Look."

He gestured to a comm screen where the incoming craft had broadcast instructions and a police roster.

I didn't look at the woman because a familiar name caught my eye. The pilot and team leader was a man I knew. He was older than the last time I had seen him. His eyes were no longer filled with laughter but had turned cold and frightening. The planes on his face were more angular, though a short beard hid most of his face.

His title was the most surprising. Until that moment, I had no idea he had moved up in rank so quickly or that he worked directly for the fleet president. "James Markswell, head fleet officer."

Raph looked over my shoulder. "Looks like a jerk. Do you know him?"

The light over the docking portal turned yellow at the same time that the dock clamps ground to a halt.

I flipped off the comm screen and stepped back into place. "He was my fiancé."

CHAPTER FOUR

Raph shot me an alarmed look. "You were engaged? Please tell me it ended well."

I stared at the dock door. I was nauseated and fighting the primal part of my brain that was screaming at me to fling myself out of an airlock rather than run into the only man I had ever loved. "He was in his last year of officer training when I started my advanced flight training at Fleet University on Earth. We were planning our wedding, but right after he graduated, we got into a huge fight. He said I was cold, would never be able to love anyone, and would die alone. I said he was unmotivated, unambitious, and would be a failure at whatever he did."

"Well, everyone says terrible things during a fight."

"He sent me every gift I had ever given him with a note saying that I could use the items to try and fool another man into thinking I was a human with real emotions before destroying their life."

Raph winced. "Maybe he regrets that because you were more mature?"

"I sent back his engagement ring. I called it a tiny handcuff and suggested he use it to shackle another woman as his marital slave."

"Well, it's been nice working for you. I'll write you in jail."

The light over the door turned from yellow to green, and the airlock hissed as the pressure stabilized. A million thoughts raced through my brain, but they were too quick to identify beyond flashes. Studying together in the library. Getting cupcakes at my favorite bakery after I aced my last final and officially was top of my class. Him telling me that I was the love of his life as he gave me a thin platinum band. In the pass of a heartbeat, the corner where I had buried it all was a violent jumble of emotions, good and bad.

Raph cleared his throat, just a little verbal nudge for me, and I pulled in a breath.

I re-centered, locking away a lifetime of pain as I slammed the door on my memories. I'd learned the skill after my parents' deaths and perfected it during the trial. By the time James stood in front of me, after ducking slightly and turning to slide his body through the small doorframe, I knew that even an expert wouldn't be able to detect any discomfort or distress in my expression.

James was older, but it was more than that. All his angles had sharpened and hardened. He appeared to be chiseled from stone, unyielding and dense. Even without our history, I would not want to face off against him. When our eyes met, I didn't flinch, but a shot of electricity went through me.

He didn't recognize me, or at least, that was the impression he gave. But he would need to be a moron not to recognize my name and face, and he had never been that. I had expected to read something in his ice-cold blue eyes, but they were as slick and unchanging as a glacier.

We stood there, looking at each other like strangers, until a second officer stepped through the doorway. All the reactions I had been holding back came out in a gasp of surprise that would have been obvious to James if he hadn't also turned to face her.

She looked exactly like me, or at least, she looked like I did when I had been engaged to James. The shape of her face was different from mine with a longer and narrower nose, and she had fair skin. But the heavy eyeliner winged out with a smoky-bronze eyeshadow, red lips, and thick eyebrows matched the look I had worn at the academy on Earth. But it was the hair that really stood out, buzzed short on the sides and longer on top, all bleached to blinding white except the tips, which were violet.

It had been an expensive time-absorbing look to maintain. Next to the hair, my brown skin, often called "nicely tanned" by people who didn't realize it was my natural shade, looked off without the full face of makeup to compensate and complete the look. It was a costume that I wore to hide my insecurity, and it had worked until everything fell apart.

I still had the look when I had gone public to defend my uncle and when I had been dubbed Lying Liz by the media. After the truth was revealed, even to me, I had to give up so much, almost everything, that a shift in appearance seemed minor.

During the trial, I had grown out my hair and let my natural warm-brown color return. When that happened, I could dial back the makeup and feel comfortable in my own skin even as the world crumbled around me.

She turned to look me in the eyes, and all the hatred I had expected from James, I found in her. If looks could kill, she would have shot me into a black hole to be torn apart at the atomic level.

She raised her upper lip in a snarl before turning back to James, her expression falling into full adoration. My stomach twisted as I realized how much the scene looked like a picture I had of James and me together. I had left my photos on Earth along with most of my physical possessions, but the image was etched into my brain. She didn't look exactly like me, but there was a strong resemblance.

I could practically feel the hairs on the back of my neck rise. Why on earth would she make herself look like that? I watched them, the space between them, the angle of her body, the tip of her chin, and the way a smile sneaked up on her lips. She was in love with him.

I thought things were already at the worst possible stage, but I was wrong. Watching my ex-fiancé with my replacement was a great way to take the situation up a notch.

I couldn't stand it any longer. I had to say something. "Hello, James."

Officer Girlfriend narrowed her eyes at me, shifting her brown contacts to show the blue underneath, but she didn't spew whatever venom was on the tip of her tongue.

James's expression was neutral. He set his feet wide in a power stance. "Please refer to me as Senior Officer Markswell. Captain Elizabeth Laika, your crew was ordered to stay in their quarters."

Next to me, Raph bristled, so I twisted my hand and touched his forearm. It was a slight movement that I hoped James didn't notice. Raph had opened his mouth to speak but snapped it shut.

I stepped forward. "Navigator Raphael Johnson was present when the fatality was discovered and wanted to offer his perspective."

"It is not his job to determine when he will be interviewed. I'll be noting this deliberate disregard in my report, and—"

I interrupted. "Oh, James. You know—"

"I *said* to refer to me as Senior Officer Markswell." Anger was slipping out from behind his calm, formal façade.

Something in that set off the bubble of unease in me, and it burst into white-hot rage. "Senior Officer Markswell, I request and require you to return to your shuttle until your remaining support staff arrive, an event which must occur within the next fourteen hours from our first point of contact. When your team boards, I will be filing for an executive lawyer to be present."

James didn't react, but I could see the muscle in his jaw working. He must have forgotten the fact that I was the one who had spent weeks quizzing him for his final exam on fleet investigations. I didn't have a photographic memory, but it was pretty darn good, especially when the case law could potentially affect me. Not that I ever thought I would be on the wrong end of one of his investigations.

I clenched my right fist down at my side. "Based on our history, I should be requesting a new lead law enforcement officer."

"Fine! You made your point, Liz. But I want it understood that if you do anything to tamper with the investigation, I will call your bluff."

I looked him square in the eyes. "And I will call yours. Someone died on my ship. I want justice served as much as you do. *James*."

He sighed. "Where is the communications room? Officer Halston and I will collect the records. This ship is under quarantine until we've finished that section of the investigation. That means that you and your navigator will both need to stay in your rooms."

The tension shattered, leaving Raph and Officer Girlfriend to size up the opposition. If they were dogs, they would have been straining at their leashes and growling.

Officer Halston spoke up. "James, should I escort them? Make sure they don't try anything?" She probably intended to sound menacing, but she didn't.

His eyes cut to her, and she flinched. He hated either having his instructions questioned or her using his first name, probably both. Whatever the reason, it gave me a spark of satisfaction.

I turned to leave, Raph falling neatly into place at my side. Our footsteps echoed on the industrial metal flooring. When the ship had been new, it was slick. But time changed everything, and the loose panels magnified the sounds of us treading across them.

Once we were out of hearing range, I nodded. "Thank you for joining me. It was nice to present a united front." I hoped that said enough.

"Permission to speak freely, Cap?"

I was so surprised by his formal request that I faltered before recovering my pace. "Of course."

"I don't trust him. Or her. Them. The whole danged fleet. It feels even more like a setup now that I've seen him. He has secrets."

"We all have secrets. He'll do a good job."

"The man you were engaged to might have, but people change."

I knew the truth of that more than anyone else. "I see your point. I'll be cautious."

CHAPTER FIVE

By the time quarantine was lifted, my stomach was ready to head out on its own to find food. It shouldn't have taken so long to download the records and seal off the crime scene.

I entered the mess hall on autopilot. To my right was the ordering station piled high with prepared food and a section for custom orders normally programmed in ahead of time, though I imagined most of the crew was going to have last-minute comfort-food requests from the food producer.

Despite my stomach's desires, it was my heart that needed to be fed, so I veered left to the large bank of windows that encompassed the entire wall. The ship was old and decrepit, but sometime in the past, it had been a leader in its field. Though the rest of the ship had aged, the full wall of windows was the reason the ship had been such a good home to me.

I stared out, and it was like my heart started beating again. The richness of space was a welcome friend, and I let out a breath I hadn't realized I was holding. My shoulders lowered, and as I cranked my neck left and right, my spine cracked.

The Night Horse galaxy looked back at me, the same and yet a living constellation that was always slightly different: rotating, galaxying, and shifting around for all eternity. It had been dancing long before I was born and would continue long after I was no more.

There was no place that I felt as small and insignificant and yet perfectly at peace and close to God. Space had been my one constant friend since childhood, and I cherished every opportunity to stare out into it. The only other place that had a window near this size was the navigation room. But that was all business, and this was all pleasure.

I could stand in the center, and my entire field of view would be filled with stars and planets. It was almost as though the ship ceased to exist and it was just me and the universe. If I didn't need my own room to metaphorically lick my wounds, I would have spent every minute in the mess hall, staring off into the distance.

I spun around to face someone who was approaching quickly from my right. My body moved on instinct before my brain fully noticed what was happening. I had years of military training, but I was clearly out of practice since Chloe was practically on top of me.

"Easy. No need to get your knickers in a knot." She handed me a cookie the size of my face then bit into her own half-eaten one.

I took a bit of the peanut butter delight while casting a look over my shoulder. It was chewy and sweet with a bit of crunch on the outside. It was just what I needed. "Thank you, but make sure the investigating team doesn't see these."

"Raph told me the guy is a real jerk and you dated him." She finished off her cookie and wiped her hands on her pants. There were deep orange smudges under her eyes, and her gills twitched.

"Don't worry. He's good at what he does. You can't even get into advanced officer training unless you have a sterling record. He can be a real pain in the neck, but he will find out who killed the Cerulean and why."

"But Raph says that Officer Markswell was really mad at you." Chloe twisted her hands.

"Raph's being cautious, and I already promised I would be careful. I will call in legal counsel if necessary, but don't worry. It won't be necessary."

"It's not just that. It's the Ceruleans. They are hiding things as well. I think... I don't trust them."

I let out a little sigh. "Chloe, you are getting all worked up for no reason. I'm going to talk to Raph as well. There is no reason for anyone to be jumping to conclusions."

She shook her head. "I'm not jumping to anything. I talked to the Ceruleans myself. Something is off."

"Chloe," I said in a warning tone.

"A member of their party was murdered, and they had been under quarantine. It was appropriate that I made sure they were comfortable and provide any provisions they needed. That's my job, after all."

"Of course, you're correct. Since you already spoke to them for official reasons, did you discover anything?" I bit into the cookie.

Sugar wasn't allowed on ship because it was too addictive and without any nutritional content, but I had long looked the other way when Chloe used it for baking. Life was more than nutritional value. Sometimes you needed a bit of harmless joy to make life worth living, especially given the drudgery of transporting cargo.

"They're hiding something, and I think I know what." She leaned in, dramatically smiling. "I think the future princess is traveling incognita to her wedding."

"Princess? On this ship?" I snorted. "Must not be a very rich planet."

Cerulea was one of the planets roughly along the path we traveled, and I had a vague sense it was a smaller planet. With hundreds of inhabited planets in the current sector, I was not versed in all of them as that was a specialized area of study. But something wasn't lining up.

Chloe confirmed my hunch. "They are very rich and snobby. They seldom leave the planet, which was what got me suspicious. I knew the royal wedding was coming up, and the princess had been off-planet for some time. They currently have a king, and when he marries, the bride will be a princess. I noticed the way everyone was deferring to the tall female in the pink dress, and I am almost positive I recognize her. I used some of my data credits to search for a picture and found one from when she left the planet. I'm pretty sure it's her." Chloe held up her work unit and pressed a few buttons then turned the screen to show me.

I looked across the room at where the four Ceruleans were at a table. Their blue skin varied slightly in tone. There was a tall dark-blue female sitting next to a small man with Earth-sky-blue skin. In the middle shades were a smaller female and a tall man. I observed the interactions between them to try to see what I could discern.

The smaller female busied herself with arranging items on the table, constantly looking to the other female for feedback. The taller female occasionally acknowledged the smaller one but mostly seemed to be listening to the males, who were arguing, or at least discussing, a topic with great enthusiasm. Their gestures were abrupt, and they talked over each other.

If they were fleet members, I would have guessed the tallest female and male were roughly peers and the two shorter ones were lower ranked. But it was dangerous to make assumptions about cultures from other societies, especially those from isolated planets without a significant fleet presence. They could often have standards that were quite literally alien to our understanding.

I looked at the picture and back at the tall female. Her hair was styled slightly differently, but it had the same bluish-black color that reminded me of an Earth raven's wings. It was pulled back severely, and picturesque little locks framed her face.

The eyes in the picture had thick and slightly even black surrounding them. I guessed it to be eye makeup, which wasn't present on the female at the table, but the general shape of the eyes, face, and lips seemed to be the same. Given how different the smaller female appeared and the variation of the males, the match between the picture and the female seemed even more conclusive.

I handed the work unit back to Chloe. "I'm not convinced, but I can't deny that the taller female does look like the picture. Did you spend all your data credits to get it?"

I heard that there was a time when all of Earth's knowledge was available with the pressing of a few keys. How little they must have known, and how little they had explored space. The ship carried a large amount of information, but I doubted that Cerulean royalty nuptials had made the cut. Transferring information off of and onto the cargo ship was severely limited, and most crew waited to be docked on the planet where they could receive more information in a few hours, depending on how many lightyears away the data was stored. Transferring data through intraspace was often slower than flying it there via a ship.

"I had to use all my credits and borrow some of Raph's, but I'm pretty sure this was worth it. The future princess is apparently a wild child, and they feared she wouldn't return at all. They've been worrying for the past year."

I tipped my head to the side. "How do you know all this?"

"I've watched every season of *True House Mavens of Cerulea*. Raph gets me the episodes through a guy he knows."

"Please tell me that is an educational documentary."

"No." She jutted her chin up in the air. "It's a reality show and a lot of fun."

I leaned in. "You know that isn't allowed."

She blew out a breath. "Nothing is allowed. Sugar, good shows, fiction books that aren't deemed educational. And don't tell me that you don't know what I am talking about because I know—"

"Fine!" I threw up my hands.

"I know you don't care, or I wouldn't do it," Chloe said seriously. "But we both know the fleet is getting out of control. Anyways, I've been watching the show for years, and the future princess returning to marry the king has been a big storyline this season. I can't believe she's here. I'm surprised they don't have cameras."

"Or a bigger security detail? Why are they *here*? Why not someplace fancier?" I chewed on my lower lip.

"Are you going to finish that cookie?" Chloe bounced on her toes, her gills flapping in anticipation.

I broke the cookie in half and handed her one side. "Tell me everything you know."

She smiled and bit into the cookie. After swallowing, she took a deep breath for what promised to be some epic info. "The king is *mostly* a figurehead that dictates styles, customs, and entertainment. You know that entertainment is one of their chief exports."

"An entire planet can survive on reality shows?"

"Maybe, but it's more than that. They also export these items made of this gorgeous material, but I think it is mostly reality shows, books, and all that awesome stuff."

"Are their immigration treaties strict? Why don't more people live there?"

"It isn't weird to see a foreigner but not super common either. I've heard it's a hot destination for most planet hoppers. This marriage has been set up for about a decade, but five years ago, the princess went off-planet to be educated—fashion design, I believe, since she will be responsible for setting all the future styles. She was supposed to return last year, but the excuses started piling up. She had a cold. There was a sandstorm on whatever dusty planet she was on. The holidays were making it impossible to leave."

I bit into my cookie and rolled my hand in the universal "go on" gesture.

"Rumors were starting to fly that something was wrong, and a date was set for the wedding with an only-so-slightly veiled threat that if she didn't arrive, then someone else would step up. Let me tell you that was all anyone talked about for weeks! All the House Mavens on the show were planning their outfits and gifts. I'm not sure about the date because they use a different calendar, but if she is traveling to Cerulea, then the wedding must be within the week." Chloe squealed.

I frowned. "None of that explains why she would be on this ship."

"I was getting to that. Her whole journey to the castle, and yes, he has a legit castle like someone out of a fairy tale with a moat and everything. I mean it is—"

"Chloe, focus."

She shook her head. "Sorry, I'll tell you about that later. You should come over and see it. Maybe there's a *clue*. So the whole journey to her wedding is steeped in tradition. She has to take the most humble means of travel to her parents' house. Everywhere else on the continent, there are parties and festivals, but she has to fast and do some cleansing ritual. Then she takes this rickety old train to the castle. It's all symbolic about her shedding her old life and embracing the new life. So romantic." Chloe clutched her hands to her chest and sighed.

I looked around the room. The paint was faded from the rich blue it had been decades earlier into an anemic pale blue. An overhead light in the corner flickered constantly, and there was even rust around the sink where the crew were supposed to wash their hands before eating. *Rust!* Travel on this freighter certainly qualified as humble means. "I'm not sure how romantic it is especially with a murder. Who was he?"

"I don't know. I don't know any of them, besides the

future princess."

I squinted a little, trying to make my view of her fuzzy and mentally overlaying the picture that Chloe had shown me. "If that's her at all."

"Why don't you go over there and find out?"

I bit the corner of my lip. James would figure it out, and if not him then the forensic team that he would surely call in. But it was my ship, dumpy, broken, and old but still mine. "Do you have any more cookies?"

She nodded, and I followed her to the kitchen while I put together a plan of what to say when I approached them. Before exiting the kitchen, I took a few slow, deep breaths and yawned. It was a trick I had learned from James, of all people. It fooled your body into thinking you were relaxed even when you weren't.

I had done it hundreds of times in the past to seem cool and collected before big meetings, recorded appearances, and even my own trial. I hadn't done it recently, but like a well-worn shoe, I hadn't forgotten the process, and confidence settled on my shoulders like a mantle.

I approached the table, a tray of cookies in hand. One at a time, the Ceruleans noticed my approach and quieted. Eventually, the princess glanced at me.

I tipped my head in a respectful greeting. "I'm Captain Laika. I apologize that your journey has been interrupted by troubles. I bring a traditional food gift." I slid the tray onto the table.

The taller female Cerulean inclined her head toward me. "You may call me Vanessa. Please take a seat and drink with us." She gestured to a chair and slid a teacup filled with dark-brown liquid toward me.

Vanessa was probably not her given name, but many chose a "fleet name" to use when off their home worlds. At the very least, the pronunciation had been altered for UL tongues. It was partially a reflection of their opinion that fleet members weren't talented enough nor intelligent enough to pronounce their birth names correctly, but maybe some of it was just the fun of picking a name in Universal Language that they felt represented themselves better than whatever name they had been saddled with by their parents. Or maybe it was her real name, and I was projecting assumptions.

I took the offered tea, but before I could sit, I was interrupted by a gruff male voice.

"Captain Laika, I would like to speak to you in private."

CHAPTER SIX

I followed James and Officer Halston to my quarters for our interview. I'd known it was coming, though the timing wasn't ideal. I had submitted a detailed account of what had happened with headquarters when I reported the unattended death, but I knew that James would need to conduct his own interview.

When we reached my quarters, I realized with a start that I was still carrying the tea, so I dumped it into the plant that stood to the side of my door as I entered. The thing was practically immortal, which was what I most desired in a plant and explained why it hadn't already died.

I sat on the edge of the bed and pointed at a chair placed near the porthole. I had arranged the area so I could read on my large recreation tablet and gaze out into space. The cushion had a deep indent, and I smirked a little when James sat and slowly sank down with his knees being pushed into his chest. There was no place left for Officer Halston to sit, so she leaned against the wall.

"Liz, you have to be honest," James said. "If you killed the Cerulean in self-defense, it is best that you come clean immediately."

It took me a few moments to gather my thoughts and

reply. "I didn't kill him in self-defense or otherwise."

"Does someone have something over you? Threatening you? You know that coercion is an extenuating circumstance."

"What are you talking about? I told the home office what happened."

"Please, Liz, I want to help you out of whatever situation you have gotten yourself into."

I stood up. "I haven't gotten myself into any situation. This is ridiculous. Are you saying that you think I had something to do with the Cerulean's murder?"

Heather pushed away from the wall and intercepted me, blocking my view of James. "We know what you've done, and I intend to prove it, which shouldn't be hard. You left evidence everywhere."

I looked her up and down then stepped around her to face James. "Is this some kind of good-cop-stupid-cop situation?"

I had kept some of my attention on Heather and for good reason. As soon as I finished speaking, she lunged at me with a hiss.

I twisted my body low into a crouch, pushing one shoulder in her direction. She hadn't expected that and was moving too quickly to adjust. Her arms were extended, probably to grab at me, but it left her entire midsection exposed. I body-checked her lower stomach, the power of my legs propelling me. She deflected off my shoulder, her training kicking in far too late. She bounced off my bed and hit the floor.

James reacted only a split second after I did and was already between us by the time she stopped rolling. I had moved out of instinct refined by years of practice. Much of that training had taken place during the time James and I were dating.

I was breathing heavily, my stance low and wide and my hand out, ready to take on whatever threat came next.

"Officer Halston!" James barked at her while also

grabbing her hand and jerking her to her feet. "Go to the navigation room and check on the downloading data."

She stared at him, her face turning red from either embarrassment or anger. I guessed both. She had lost her temper and been thrown down on her butt then was being kicked from the room. If I was a better person, I would have felt bad for her.

But my smirk was wiped off my face the second the door closed behind her, and I remembered what we had been discussing. I looked at James, really studied his face. There was an odd sense of familiarity with him that wanted to return despite my own reluctance. He was a man that I had trusted and loved. He knew me better than probably anyone in all the universes, but like so many in my life, he had turned his back on me.

"James, I don't know what you are thinking, but I had nothing to do with the Cerulean's murder, and I can't possibly understand why you could think otherwise."

He sat in on the edge of the seat. "People don't change. The Liz I knew would never let her ship fall into such disrepair. I looked over the information, and practically none of the door sensors work. We can't get any record of who was where and when. That is the most basic level of security, and not having it work is pure negligence."

Adrenaline was still coursing through my veins, and I paced the room, hoping to walk it off. "You don't understand. This ship is old. It's held together through sheer luck and the work of an amazing crew. Headquarters wants no part in helping me, and I've gotten along fine without them so far."

He perked up a little. "You requested to have these things repaired, and they refused?"

"I did once, but they refused, and I got the message."

"What message?" His eyebrows pulled together in genuine curiosity.

"That I was on my own out here."

"That is not how the fleet functions. There is no hold

on your ship. If you needed repairs, you just needed to submit them."

My fingernails dug painfully into my palm as I clenched my hands into fist. "You know nothing of how things work. I may have been declared innocent in the eyes of the court, but as far as he's concerned, I'm guilty."

"He who?"

"Your boss, the fleet president."

"You think he has a personal vendetta against you? That's why you didn't get your ship repaired? You sound paranoid."

A sensation like molten lava rolled through my stomach, making me want to hurl or punch him. Maybe both. I *really* wanted to punch him. "I'm not paranoid!" My voice cracked, and I knew that I was just proving his point. I turned away. "You don't understand."

"The Liz I knew would fight for her ship and crew. You could have filed a formal complaint, and—"

"The old Liz is dead!"

"People don't change that much."

I spun around, hoping the tears in my eyes weren't visible. "Everything changes." I suddenly felt so exhausted that I wasn't sure if my legs could hold my weight much longer. I collapsed on the bed, willing to take whatever he had to dish out.

He stood and went to the window. "If you killed him, I will do whatever I can to make sure you have a fair trial. But I can't understand what's going on if you don't tell me."

I let out a long sigh. "I didn't kill him."

He sighed in reply and turned to me, his face one of a stranger. "We did a ship scan, and the only weapons that came up were what you and your navigator carry. We found your pajamas covered in your own blood and some of his. Your fingerprints are all over the victim's room. Did he attack you?"

A bark of laughter escaped my lips. "Is that what you're

37

worried about? I can't tell you about the weapon other than that you missed something. But the rest is easy to explain. Raph and I were in the navigation room when I was notified of the situation. We jogged down there. I tripped over a loose panel and landed on a jagged piece of metal, ripping my pajamas. I lost quite a bit of blood from the wound. I had it taken care of, then we went to the room, where I determined the Cerulean was deceased, and I called it in."

The muscle in James's jaw was flexing, and he closed his eyes briefly while taking a deep breath. "I'll just start at the beginning. Why were you in your pajamas?" He pulled a thin tablet from the pocket on the side of his pants, unfolded it, and removed a stylus.

I went through the whole story of our midnight refueling. He jotted notes as I talked, to go along with the automatic recordings. I had to assume that all my interactions with him would be reviewed eventually.

He looked up, his pen posed in midair. "There is no record of any medical treatment being dispensed. Based on the amount of your blood we found, there should have been."

I debated lying for only the smallest of fractions of a second, but even as I did, I knew I was going to tell the truth even at the risk of lowering James's opinion of me yet again. "A crew member broke protocol and handled it himself." I fidgeted with my clothing, eventually exposing the jagged wound, which was healing nicely despite the seared-meat appearance and deep-purple bruising.

He paled slightly and turned away to cough before continuing. "So I suppose that's why we found your blood in the victim's room and his blood on your clothing?"

"I suppose so. I didn't realize I'd gotten his blood on me. I went into the room and…" I remembered a detail that hadn't been in the report and grimaced. "And I passed out. All that blood plus my own injury and pain, I guess it was too much."

He grunted but didn't question me. He probably remembered the time I'd passed out while attempting to donate blood. It had been humiliating to show such a visible sign of weakness when I felt that I was otherwise at the top of my game. I was no longer at the top of any game, but it was obvious my ego was still capable of being bruised.

I pushed ahead to another point. "I probably got my blood everywhere and picked up any blood that had dripped on the floor. It didn't even occur to me to say anything about it. I didn't have my work unit on me, so I used the communication portal in the victim's room, and the room was secured afterwards."

He grunted, scribbling notes before circling something on his tablet and drawing a couple of arrows.

I could feel the pressure rising in the room. Maybe I was projecting, but I was sure he was judging me, and it made my hackles rise. "I know that a lot of things I'm saying aren't exactly 'according to protocol,' but it works. We have never once had a late delivery or lost anything in transit. My crew is happy with the delivery bonuses and… happy in general."

I hadn't given the crew's emotions much thought until it was halfway out of my mouth, but by that point, I was sure I was right. I spent most nights holed up in my room, but I had noticed the laughs and easy comradery in the dining hall. Most of the crew had smiles on their faces, and though many moved on after a period of time, almost all had indicated that they enjoyed their time on my ship. It wasn't glamorous or exciting, but it wasn't miserable either. In fact, I realized with a start, I was happy on the ship as well, or at least as happy as I could be given the circumstances that held me there.

James looked up. "Liz, no one is questioning your abilities as a captain."

"Yes, you are. I can hear it just under the surface. You feel my answers aren't sufficient."

"They aren't. I don't think you realize what's at stake here. These aren't just some run-of-the-mill travelers. They are on an important mission, and there have been death threats. No one knew the details of their itinerary, and the time of travel has been kept secret from everyone. Cerulea is putting great pressure on the fleet to find the criminal, which is why it is so important that—"

I snorted loudly. "No one knows anything? Five minutes of data searching, and one of my crew members discovered that Vanessa is engaged to the king of Cerulea, and their wedding is within the week. I am sure that information will come up during your investigation of ships transactions, and you will see that it was discovered *after* the murder was already committed. I didn't know anything about who they were until then, but it would have been easy for anyone else to figure it out."

"What do you mean? Figure it out how exactly?"

"There is some big show based on Cerulea, and the upcoming wedding is a big topic. It isn't as covert as the king has led you to believe. If one of my crew members could put it together while in transit, then anyone on a planet with a dedicated data center could know in seconds."

James groaned and scrubbed his face. For a split second, I felt the urge to comfort him, but that was quickly overrode by disgust that he actually thought I could murder a passenger for either money or political favor. We had broken up, but I wasn't a monster.

"I didn't realize that. I'll be interviewing them again." Admitting that he had missed something appeared to cause him pain, though I wished I could add some literal pain to the situation.

I went to the door, which I opened to the hallway, and gestured for him to exit. "I am sure it will be very informative. And you might want to warn your little girlfriend that if she attacks me again, I won't be so gentle next time."

CHAPTER SEVEN

I gave myself a few minutes to splash some water on my face and freshen up. I didn't want to admit how rattled I'd been or how naïve I felt. I thought I had lost the last of my naïveté during my trial, but I had been disillusioned all over again.

It was my ship, and I needed to take control. Since I still hadn't eaten, I headed to the dining hall again and picked up food first. I shoveled it into my mouth as fast as I could without actually getting sick.

I was finishing up my meal when Raph entered and caught my eye. I gestured for him to join me, and before I could even say hi, he was speaking.

"Cap, I really have an uneasy feeling about this whole mess."

I nodded. "I know. You're right."

He stared at me for a second. "Oh... good. I thought Horton and I were going to have to convince you. He just left to check a reading in the engine, but he should be back any minute. He agrees with me that something is off."

"I should have listened to your gut. James and Officer Girlfriend basically accused me of being the killer."

"I knew it. What's their angle?"

"Chloe told you what she found, right?" I waited for him to confirm that he knew. "James knew as well but seemed to believe it was a big secret. He implied that I was either being paid or being blackmailed into it. He also tried to convince me to say it was self-defense, probably just to get me to admit something. He seems convinced that I am behind it."

Raph whistled. "Harsh."

"I'm not getting blamed for something I didn't do. Not again at least. I don't know if I could survive another trial." I could feel the anxiety growing in the pit of my stomach and crawling up my throat, threatening to suffocate me.

Something must have shown in my face because Raph was quick to respond. "You're not going to trial, Liz. We're going to figure this out. I know some people who owe me favors I can cash in. I'll see what I can find out. Should I be asking for any particulars?"

I twisted my seat to stare out the window. The information we had was so limited that the possibilities were endless. "I haven't gotten that far. Do you know the Ceruleans' names?"

He pulled out his work unit. "Yes, more or less. Vanessa, Wylene, Rick, and Todd. Those are all that are on the manifest. Oh, and Mike was the one who died. No other names were used, so these are either fleet names or throwaway aliases for travel."

"If all the information I have so far is correct, then Vanessa is the one that is going to marry the king, so Wylene must be the other female. Rick and Todd would be the two males. But don't assume too much without confirming. See if you can find out more... well... everything, I guess. Real names, if they have them. Where they were before this trip? What are their jobs or roles normally? Relationship to each other? Does anyone know them at the port we picked them up or the port where we were dropping them off? Cast as wide a net as necessary."

I leaned in closer. "You also might want to run a check

on all paid staff here. We have a lot of crew members transitioning in and out. That's a big ask. I'm not sure about what your contacts are going to want in exchange, but if you need—"

He held up his hand. "Don't even say it. I'll handle everything."

I let out a breath and sat back. I knew that his connections weren't always on the up-and-up, but I was backed into a corner. I hadn't imagined how good it would feel to have people in my corner, but when he offered to take care of it, no questions asked and nothing in exchange, it was as though I was inhaling a deep breath of fresh air after a long shuttle ride.

I felt lighter and brighter. "Thank you."

A strange look crossed his face. "Of course, we're a team. Hold on. Let me tell something to Chloe."

He stood up and strode across the room to disappear into the kitchen. I took the chance to take a shaky breath. I had pictured myself as alone in the world, but slowly, I had built up a team around me. I trusted Raph. Though we had started out bumpy, we had found a groove. It was the same with Chloe and Horton. They had always been honest and forthright, never letting me down without an honest explanation of why. It had happened so naturally that I hadn't realized it until then. Maybe everything would be okay after all.

A noise pulled my attention around to the entrance, where Vanessa stood with her fellow Ceruleans as they faced off against James. They caught sight of me only a few seconds after I spotted them.

The princess stepped toward me, finger outstretched in accusation as she shouted in the suddenly quiet room. "Arrest the captain. She's a murderer!"

CHAPTER EIGHT

I should have been shocked, leaping to my feet to scream my innocence, but instead, I found myself laughing.

Whatever reaction Vanessa had expected, that wasn't it, and she shifted uncomfortably before continuing her attack. "She doesn't deny it. Arrest her. Turn her over to my king for justice."

Whatever rage that skipped me seemed to have landed squarely on James's shoulders. "Stand down! This is my investigation." His face was practically scarlet, and his voice echoed in the metal room.

She turned to him with narrowed eyes. "If you could do your job properly, I would not need to do it for you. She's a criminal. We all know it. Now she's killed a passenger, and no one will do a thing about it."

I stood up slowly and started to approach her. Maybe I was in the middle of a mental breakdown, but I suddenly felt far calmer than I should have given the circumstances. "The lady doth protest too much."

She obviously wasn't familiar with Shakespeare. "What does that mean?"

James stepped in front of me. "Vanessa, you're out of

line. This is a fleet vessel, and no fleet officer will be subject to any court except our own."

It was hardly a comforting statement, but it got under Vanessa's skin. Her face turned a deeper shade of blue until it was almost black.

The younger woman placed a hand on her shoulder. "Sister, please."

The taller male stepped in front of her. "Va'nes'sa, daughter of the Venom Keeper, future wife of the king of Cerulea, future empress of communications with other planets, I must request that we leave. I will escort you to your room to rest."

With each honorific, she seemed to relax more, as if they were a balm to her soul. By the end of his litany, her face had returned to her normal shade of blue. She took his offered arm to leave.

James watched them go before turning back to me. "Does this ship go any faster?"

I had opened my mouth to answer when alarms sounded. My work unit buzzed, and a light flashed in the corner of my eye. Before I could move, the ship rocked hard to one side and flung me on James.

CHAPTER NINE

By the time I managed to get back on my feet, my gut felt twisted from the scent of James filling my nose. While I knew he was no longer the man I loved, he still tore at me.

Raph raced by, slowing just enough to shout at me, "The engine room!"

Adrenaline quickly overrode my memories. I had been thrown directly starboard. There could be a couple of reasons for that, and none were good.

I fell in step with Raph in an eerie reminder of racing to the site of the murder. Had that been twelve hours ago? Twenty-four hours? Forty-eight? Being unmoored from my schedule and in the middle of a crisis had left my handle on time a bit slippery. We followed the same path, but instead of Chloe heaving next to me, it was James. His footsteps were heavy, which wasn't surprising given his bulk.

Raph pulled ahead of us as we hit the stairs, but I refused to fall behind James while on my own ship. My side screamed, and a burning sensation that started at my not-yet-healed wound was crawling down my leg and up to my neck. A cold, clammy feeling was spreading over my face, and I was worried I might faint. When the ship rocked again, another wave of adrenaline kicked in. The alarms were still sounding, and the work unit on my leg continued to buzz, a reminder I ignored despite the fact that it would grow in frequency until I turned it off.

Whatever the alerts were saying couldn't be more urgent than the flashing lights and alarms blaring. I slid to a stop in front of the engine room, one hand on the outer wall. It was hot and getting hotter. Heat was radiating from the open door. Flames licked out of the engine grating. I could see Horton lying facedown on the floor. He was perfectly still, his skin black in the glow of the flames.

"Initiate the override!" I screamed.

Raph shouted something back, but I couldn't hear him over the alarms.

I took a step toward the door, and James grabbed my arm. "You can't go in there. Seal it and save the living."

He was right. That was proper protocol. It was too much of a risk to go in after Horton. It was a fool's errand to even try.

I shook James off and ducked through the door. Horton was part of my crew. And I wasn't leaving without him.

CHAPTER TEN

Two steps into the room, half the distance to Horton, and I knew I couldn't do it. It took everything in me to force my body to keep advancing, knowing there was no way I was going to have anything left to haul Horton out. He had to be thrice my size.

I grabbed one of his thick gnarled hands and leaned back, pulling him from the fire toward the door. The heat radiating off him made me fight my instinct to let go. I tugged him in a jerky motion, relying on my body weight to leverage him across the floor. Pain screamed through me. In the split second I had left before I collapsed, I wondered if this last heroic act would be enough to atone for my failures. Would I be remembered for this or for the crimes I didn't commit?

I fell backward when Horton's body suddenly jerked past me. A looming figure pulled him toward the door. Someone had the back of my shirt, but I was too weak to even assist in my own rescue. My lungs couldn't pull in the hot air anymore, and my limbs were dead weight.

I was a loose ragdoll as I was dragged across the floor and finally dumped out into the hallway. The door to the engine room slammed shut the moment my feet cleared the threshold. The cold air was shocking, and shaking wracked me, but the sensations were far away. My body was becoming foreign to me, and my lungs refused to move.

Time seemed to stretch and shift, reminding me of the time in training when I had experienced near-light-speed travel in an old-school rocket, the outdated method used for travel before intraspace travel was developed. The universe had expanded and contracted around me for an eternity or a thousandth of a second.

While I was in that state, a face appeared in front of me. The eyes intently stared, and a voice boomed. I knew the eyes. They were comforting and important, but I had no idea who they belonged to. I vaguely knew that the sounds meant something, but I couldn't seem to translate the noise I heard into anything understandable. A moment later, a cold mist enveloped my body, and there was a mild jolt to my system.

Slowly, my consciousness settled back into me, and the noises around me coalesced into meaning.

James barked out orders, his voice harder than I had ever heard it. "I don't care what it says. I'm shutting it all down!"

Raph appeared in my field of vision. "Hey, Cap, you gave us quite a scare. When I saw the officer pulling you and Horton out, I thought you were both dead. But we got you sorted out. Mostly."

I shifted, and every part of me from my skin down to my bones ached. My mouth tasted of garlic, a sure sign that a painkiller had been administrated. I brought my hand to my face so I could look at it. The skin was tender and hot but all there. My hand had a silver shimmer that I knew was the medication used to treat burns. I appeared to be in one piece, so I struggled to roll over and look for Horton.

Chloe was kneeling next to Horton, who lay a few feet away. His skin was black, and bits had flaked off him and lay on the metal floor. She pulled his head into her lap as she cried over him. Stroking his smooth head caused scales to float to the ground like black feathers.

"Horton," she whispered while moving the scanner over his body. The unit beeped in protest, and she growled and slammed the screen with her other hand.

Horton groaned and moved, the darkened skin splitting and sheeting off. "Oy, my head." He raised a hand to his face.

I fully rolled over and crawled to him on all fours. "Horton! Are you okay?" He turned his head toward me, but I couldn't see his amber eyes as a black cloud covered his irises.

His long, thin tongue flicked out and across each eye, removing the cataracts to reveal bright-red eyes. "I'll be okay soon enough. I just need to get to my room and molt off all the burned bits. I was overdue. I'm going to be fresh as a daisy but sore as a cracked tooth." He struggled to rise to a kneeling position, shifting around to bring his tail behind him without bending it sideways. His skin flaked off in large sheets, exposing the neon green underneath.

I had never seen him fresh from a skin shed since he used his vacation time to rest in his room, but I had previously noted that the green tint of his scales was brighter when he returned.

I was still shaky but moved to his side, overcome by guilt. "I'm so sorry, Horton. The safety override system must have malfunctioned. This is all my fault. I should have..." I let my voice fade out. I had no idea that the ship had genuine safety issues. I would have been able to overcome my concerns with contacting fleet if I had known. *Wouldn't I?*

Horton shook his head. He struggled to open his hand, which gripped a jumbled mess of metal. "It was sabotage." Finally, he let go, and the metal fell to the floor and broke apart into what I recognized as fire-blackened tools.

I picked up a wrench then dropped it when it burned my hand. "I don't understand. How do you know it was sabotage?"

"I found those stuffed into the grate of the engine. I was able to grab a few out, burned my paw something awful, but then I saw the rest of my toolbox had been thrown in too. I went over to see why the shut-down override was off. Sometimes, the ladies that clean the area turn it off on accident, but the screen was shattered. The last thing I remember was trying to make it to the hallway when something blew, and I was knocked to the ground. I thought I was a goner."

Chloe threw her arms around Horton. "Liz saved you! Then James saved you both! I thought you were both *dead.*"

"Senior Officer Markswell," snapped James. His whole face and both of his hands shimmered.

I ignored him and focused on Horton. "Are you sure?" I knew he wouldn't lie as I hadn't seen even a hint of dishonestly in him since we had been working together.

"Absolutely. I have been double- and triple-checking things since… uh… Senior Officer Markswell asked if I could get this old ship moving any faster. I did a full run of systems checks a few hours ago. Got out my tools to try some old-fashioned fiddling when Raph asked me to come to the dining hall for some grub and an important conversation. I wasn't gone more than thirty minutes."

I nodded, the facts of the situation all sliding into place in my brain. While I had, at first at least, been willing to leave the investigation to the fleet officers, my crew was at risk. This was personal.

James was also keenly interested in our exchange. "Who would have access to the engine room?"

I suppressed a groan as another wave of guilt rolled over me. "Anyone on the ship probably. The key system has been broken for…" I looked to Raph.

He shrugged. "At least twenty round trips. It was

dodgy for a dozen or so before that, so I got a friend to get a workaround. But it finally broke. Sorry to say that anyone could get in if they knew where the room was."

James's jaw shifted from side to side, which I knew meant he was in deep thought, working on a theory. I was opening my mouth to ask about what he thought when Officer Halston joined us.

She looked at my motley crew with only passing interest, which was a big step up from the normal disdain she had shown me every other time she saw me. She turned all her attention to James. "Senior Officer Markswell, I secured the remaining crew and passengers, but we have an issue."

"Get on with it," said James. "What's wrong?"

"I couldn't find the three females designated as custodial staff. I was told that they had taken tea to their rooms. I went to get them, and..." She swallowed awkwardly before continuing flatly. "They're dead."

CHAPTER ELEVEN

I paced my room, hoping that the movement of my legs would magically make my brain come up with answers. My ship was floating aimlessly in space, and James had pulled rank to lock us down in our rooms until backup could arrive to evacuate us and tow the ship to whatever docking station they wanted to use to continue the investigation.

But I wasn't going to sit around and wait. If I sat, I would go to sleep, but it wouldn't be restful. The nightmares were waiting. Even on my best night, I had dreams of being chased through crowds of people that couldn't hear me or trying to find something dearly important that was missing. Those were stressful, and I would wake to find my shoulders tied in knots.

If I could just stay up long enough, I would slide into a dreamless, exhaustive sleep. My body was screaming for it. Between the fall and my rescue attempt, pain radiated with every step. I hadn't slept well in days. Hot and cold were coming in waves as my body struggled to maintain a consistent temperature.

I needed to lie down but just not yet. I wished I had access to my work unit to study the passenger and crew lists. James had not only taken all of them but also locked out all technology from accessing the ship's computers. I should have downloaded everything earlier, but who would ever think of doing that? Connection lockouts were virtually unheard of.

I was left with just my brain to sort it out, but there were almost no details. My thoughts were ephemeral, like little birds flittering around. I needed to read something to clear my head, but instead of my tablet filled with novels, I veered to the small table next to the bed and picked up a small Bible. It was the only thing I had left from my parents.

My mother had given it to me when I had gone to Earth for advanced flight training. Dad would have given me his, but his chicken scratch filled the margins and was indecipherable. I'd laughed and taken Mom's, but if I'd known it would be the last time I would see them, I would've taken both. Or never left at all.

The Bible was small, meant to fit into a uniform. Since our uniforms had pockets on the outside of both thighs to fit a work unit, the Bible could be slipped in the opposite pocket and kept close.

I opened to a verse that had given me comfort for years, but before I could read it, there was a quick rap on my door. It seemed sneaky, if that was possible for a knock, and I ran over to answer, sliding the Bible into my pocket as I grabbed my weapon from the side console near the door.

Fleet officers had dubbed it a banana—or ban, for short—so many decades ago that the official name was all but lost. The weapon was curved metal and looked exactly like the crescent-shaped fruit but thinner. At the top of my uniform pants was a sleeve in the waistband that I could slide the ban into, which was fine when I was up and active, but when I sat in the commander chair, it dug into my hipbone. After a few weeks, it pulled my whole lower back out of alignment. I switched sides then both sides hurt, and I had finally stopped wearing it except at destinations when I wanted to be prepared.

Given the number of murders, I decided I should be cautious. I moved the dial on the ban to a setting that would stun and incapacitate but wouldn't be lethal. Pressing my thumb on it for three seconds, I locked in and activated the setting. James had said a full lockdown procedure, so only he and his law enforcement girlfriend would be able to move freely around the ship. I edged over to open the door, expecting James to have returned for more questioning but fearing it could be Officer Halston looking for another fight. They were the only two who would be able to unlock the door. It was neither. Instead, Raph and Chloe were huddled outside my door.

Raph pushed in past me. "Let us in before those dumb cops come by." He said it with such insistence that I had let him in before I even thought to question him.

I shut the door behind him and flipped the lock. "What are you doing out of your room? Wait. *How* are you out of your room?"

Chloe walked around my room, eyeing everything in sight, which only took a few seconds. "The lock in my rock has always been screwed up, so I heard when the lockdown was disengaged. I left to get Raph, and his room was unlocked too. Then we grabbed Horton." She poked her head into my bathroom. "I didn't know you had a bathtub."

Raph grabbed the chair by the window, the only place to sit other than my bed. "Horton should be here any second. He had to grab something first. We need to come up with a plan." He seemed ready to fight me if I disagreed.

I had no intention of doing that. "Great. We need to find out everything we can about the Ceruleans and the custodial crew that was killed. Where they were before this, where they are going, why they or someone sabotaged the ship? Is it to strand us here? For what purpose? Or did they intend to blow up the ship? There are so many possible answers, I don't even know where to start."

Chloe popped her head out of the bathroom, a bar of soap held under her nose. "I might be able to answer at least one of those questions." She breathed in deeply, closing her eyes. "What is this?"

I did a quick guess as how to translate. Though I was fluent in Universal Language, I didn't know every translation for all Earth plants, if there even was one. "Lilac. An Earth flower."

"Like the color?"

"I believe, at least in English, that the pale-purple color lilac is named after the flower."

Before I could say more, she disappeared then popped her head out again with a dark vial. "And this?"

I sighed as I had no idea how to translate Vitamin C. "It's a liquid extracted from oranges and other citrus fruit. I put the liquid on my skin to keep it healthy."

"Oranges?"

"A fruit. Very good on a hot day."

"So all your colors come from fruits and flowers? Fascinating. What a strange little planet you have."

I was growing impatient. "Not all colors and this is just English, one language from Earth. You can have both if you just get out here and explain what you meant when you said, 'I can answer at least one question.'"

She slid the bar of soap and the vial into her pocket and headed over to press her face against my window. "I heard them talking when they took me to my room to lock me in. He didn't realize how good my hearing is and— there! Come here and look."

I went over to stand next to her and attempted to follow her gaze all the way under the ship to a red planet looming rather close. "The red planet? Is that what you're pointing at?"

"That's Cerulea. I thought it would be blue like them. Dumb, huh? That is why your ex is so nervous. He was sure that is why the ship was incapacitated, though he didn't use that word. I didn't think fleet officers were supposed to curse like that on duty."

I grunted in reply, unable to spare any word when my brain was chewing over that information. When combined with Vanessa's accusations, it seemed anything but coincidental that the ship was stopped here. Had my ship been picked with the idea of targeting me in mind, or was it happenstance? I had been so concerned about old grudges with the fleet that it had never occurred to me that a foreign government might have their own plans.

I turned away from the window too quickly, and black dots danced across my vision. I threw out a hand to brace myself until my vision slowly returned.

Raph moved to my side. "You okay, Cap?"

I nodded. "Fine. But I should probably rest soon. This is a bit more exciting than my normal life. This sounds weird, but we should probably look into… me. After the trial, there were some people pretty upset that I was found not guilty and… I don't know. This feels personal."

There were three quick knocks on the door. I gestured toward the bathroom. "Go hide in there."

Chloe obeyed, probably eager to rifle through the rest of my toiletries, but Raph hung back. "Why? It's probably Horton."

"Or it could be James, and do you want to explain why you're out of your room?"

"I didn't unlock the doors," he countered.

I sighed. "Just do it as a favor to me. Plus you can spy on us."

His eyes lit up. He went into the bathroom and closed the door most of the way behind him.

I opened the door with less caution than I should have, and things happened very quickly. A stunner beam hit me, and my whole body seized up. I fell down and knocked over the plant by my door, the fragile dead leaves breaking and cutting into my cheek as I lay on the floor. Everything faded to black.

CHAPTER TWELVE

Awareness came slowly, like a sunrise on Earth. I was cautious and confused, and my whole body hurt. My time on Earth had been spent in heavy training, but my current source of discomfort was not immediately obvious to me. I was shoved into a corner on a seat, my neck at an odd angle. The pain of moving was only exceeded by the continued pain of not adjusting my position.

I sat up as my muscles screamed in protest after hours of being locked into the slightly unnatural position. I used my left hand to steady myself only to realize that my hands were taped together, as were my feet. That was when my brain decided to kick into gear and replay my last few conscious moments.

I had been on my ship and stunned by... someone, but the list of possible suspects wasn't very long. I had a good guess who was involved. I remembered the sight of a ban before everything went black. There were better weapons available, so the reasons were limited as to why someone would use a fleet standard-issue weapon in a kidnapping.

And it was a kidnapping. There was not a circumstance I could imagine in which this was on the up-and-up. I twisted and stretched as best I could despite the screaming muscles and pins-and-needles sensation attacking my limbs.

It was a small room with a door that appeared to slide back into the wall. There was a little basin with a faucet on a podium. I moved my hands under my seat and pulled up on the thick cushion underneath me. It pivoted upward, confirming my suspicion. I might not have been in this exact model of shuttle, but I recognized a bathroom when I saw one.

Considering that they had stuck me in there, either they planned on an uncomfortable ride or they weren't going too far. This design of a bathroom that could serve as an extra seat was most often used in short-range shuttles for traveling from a disabled ship to a nearby planet... Cerulea, perhaps.

I set to work loosening my hands, which wasn't difficult. They were poorly tied, and the tape was already peeling. Next, I freed my feet. I stood up as much as possible in the cramped quarters and moved a little to get the blood flowing. No sooner had I started moving than the turbulence increased, in addition to the general noise in the cabin.

We were probably starting to break though the atmosphere. I wasn't sure of the exact makeup of Cerulea, but it was safe to assume that we would be landing soon. At that point, I would face my kidnappers and... what? They probably planned to pin the murder on me, but to what end? Immediate execution? Public trial? A quick death and burial in a hole?

I checked my pockets, hoping against hope that my work unit or ban were still on me, though it was as I suspected. I hadn't taken either with me to the door. I did have my mother's Bible, which was a great comfort but probably of little practical use unless I could somehow convince my captors of their grievous sins and encourage them to repent.

Frankly, that was as good a plan as any, so I set that up

as Plan A and started working on a backup plan. The interior of the door was smooth except for a sheered-off bolt halfway up on the left side. The handle had probably been knocked off before I was deposited in there so that I couldn't escape. Bummer for them. Replacement parts were notoriously difficult to acquire, and after kidnapping the captain responsible for package delivery, it was going to be quite a wait to get a new one.

And what about James and the fleet? Would they even know I was kidnapped? Or would they think that I'd escaped? Surely Raph and Chloe knew something was wrong, but would James believe them? Maybe fleet would play it off as though I was guilty, and the whole thing would be brushed under the rug. Or maybe that was their plan all along. A chill ran through me. I might really be all on my own.

The ship swung hard, and I slammed into a wall. I flopped down on the seat that converted to a toilet and noticed a drawer in the podium. Pulling it open, I saw an assortment of junk. There was a rod with protruding metal bristles, an empty tub that—based on the congealed substance in one small corner—once had contained a red liquid, and two flat metal sticks that were welded together on one side.

The brush might be able to do some damage if I swung it directly at someone's face, but I was going to need to rely heavily on the element of surprise for that approach. I ignored the empty tub but grabbed the little metal tool. It roughly resembled tweezers if one needed to pluck hair the toughness of wire.

I turned off the light in case the cabin had already been darkened. I pushed the two metal pieces into the space around the sheared-off handle then tried to grasp the bolt to twist it. It slipped on the smooth surface until I was able to catch the smallest edge of a ridge where the sheared metal had distorted. The leverage was poor, and like those in many shuttles I had been in, the latch was stiff.

Eventually, I was able to unhook it enough to break the seal on the door.

There was only the smallest sliver of space between the edge of the door and the jamb. The noise level in the bathroom instantly changed as the soundproofing was cancelled. The dull rush of white noise lowered, and the shuttle's clanks and rumbles filled the air. I worked my jaw, and my ears popped. I pressed my eye to the opening.

Based on the size of the bathroom, I had a hunch about what to expect, and sure enough, the layout I could see matched my expectations. The bathroom was tucked into a far back corner behind a row of seats, and little else was visible, not even a window that might help me judge our rate of descent.

Something was tied in front of the door, and when I attempted to wiggle the door, it caught. I guessed a rope was tied from the exterior handle to something as insurance should I manage to get the door open. Considering I had done just that, it showed they were smart.

And if I had been able to exit the bathroom, what then? I could hardly leap out an exterior door to freedom. Well, I could, and I would be gloriously free for whatever time it took me to plummet to my death or, if we were still in space, to suffocate. Both delightful choices.

I could try to fight everyone present and attempt to gain control of the shuttle. I took a moment to snort at the idea. I had handled Officer Girlfriend, but she had a messy attack that even a child could have seen coming.

A flash of two bodies passed by at a quick pace. I ducked down, even though I was reasonably sure they couldn't see me since I could see them through only the tiniest sliver.

Wylene was speaking to Vanessa in a soft, lilting foreign language when Vanessa cut her off with a stomp of her foot.

"No, sister. You'll speak Universal Language to me."

Wylene pulled back as though struck. "But we always spoke like this at home. I want to talk to you privately."

Vanessa rolled her eyes. "That is not my home any longer and never will be again with its dirty ocean air and venom farming. Once I am married, I will travel constantly. It is my freedom."

Wylene leaned forward imploringly. "I don't understand why we left the ship. We could have just waited until—"

"Do not question me and the decisions I've made. It will be like Jonah. I will be queen and have all that I desire and leave this burning red planet."

"How can you speak of Cerulea that way? The hills and curves are gorgeous. The king has large pools. He is proud and mighty. Anyone would be lucky to be his mate."

"There are other pools. Better pools. And he is of no matter to me. I will perform my duty but with no joy." She stepped forward and grabbed her sister by the arms. "Trust me. When I left, you were a girl and I but a young woman. Now, we are both women, and we know things."

"I know nothing." Wylene's face shifted to a deep blue color, and she looked away.

"Then stay by me, and I will teach you what our mother never did. It will be okay."

"And if God is with her?"

"There is always a backup plan, little sister. Trust no one but me. We must sit down as we will land soon."

"Wait!" Wylene grabbed Vanessa's arm and pulled something out of a pocket in her robe. "I asked you to come back so I could give this to you as you requested. But how could you go through so much so quickly? You never drank the tea at home. You promise you didn't abuse it?" She passed over a small container.

"Just trust me and don't ask questions," Vanessa said as her voice faded away.

The shuttle shifted, and the rumbling changed frequency. I had only a few minutes, so if I was going to form a plan, now was the time.

My options were severely limited. I had a brush with metal bristles, a pair of tweezers, and my brain. And frankly all three of those things were pretty busted. I was about to land on a planet I knew nothing about, surrounded by individuals who only wanted the worst for me.

But if I was going out, I was going out fighting. I crouched behind the door and armed myself as best I could. When they came to get me, I would come out swinging. If I was lucky and they underestimated me, I might be able to escape and run.

CHAPTER THIRTEEN

As the hours ticked by, my plan lost its appeal. Once we landed, everything shut down except the axillary lights. The shuttle was running on standby power with cool air blowing from the vent. But I was sure everyone had left. Without me. My plan was pretty harebrained, but theirs seemed ridiculous. Why kidnap me just to leave me here?

Eventually, footsteps and furtive whispering approached. Perhaps they had hoped I would fall asleep or even die. I had hit the floor pretty hard. Whatever their logic, they were back. The way they moved and the darkness of the ship meant that I couldn't see how many individuals had come, their builds, or even what language they were speaking.

I again crouched into my ready position despite my thighs screaming in pain. My workout routine was thorough but no match for hours in a squat position. A dark hand pushed the door open. I sprang up with my metal-bristled-brush weapon, ready to rake the eyes of whoever was there.

Three things happened all at once: I recognized my opponent. Chloe whispered, "Liz, No!" And I crashed into Raph, who hit the doorjamb and bounced off.

A second later, we both landed on the floor. Fortunately, he broke my fall. I would have felt bad except I was sure that if I had one more hard landing, my brain would be a scrambled egg. Raph was lanky and bony but quite a step up from bare flooring.

Chloe pulled me close, folding me in a hug. "I can't believe we found you."

I returned the hug briefly then reached out to Raph to pull him up. I would love an extended greeting, but the turn of events meant there was more intel needed. "We're on Cerulea?"

Raph answered in a slightly strained voice. "Yes. Sorry we didn't get here sooner—"

"You got here at all. That's what matters. You have the ship's shuttle?" All fleet vessels had a shuttle, though I was sure that ours was being held together with tape and hope.

Raph nodded. "We took the officer's shuttle."

He meant he had stolen it, but it was no time for quibbling. I headed for the exit at the front of the shuttle, staying close to the wall. "What was the situation out there? Guards? How do we get out of here?"

Raph was close behind me, a hand light on my shoulder as we were taught. By maintaining contact, we could move more easily in a hostile environment, like a kidnapping vehicle. "No one. We parked outside the gate, but there are shuttles everywhere. It appears to be a landing station. No one even looked twice."

I stopped so suddenly that Raph pressed his hand down on my shoulder to prevent him from running into me. A second later I heard a loud *oomph* from Chloe as she plowed into him.

Something wasn't sitting well with me, and I was fighting the twin urges to stop and think versus run and escape. I had been left in a shuttle, alone and unguarded, that was only in low-energy mode. Prickles of unease ran down my back even as my feet twitched to run.

"It's all too easy, Cap." Raph's voice was tight in the

darkness.

"Why aren't we moving? We have to get out of here." Chloe's tone was verging on hysterical, and I could hear her gills flapping.

"I know." I replied to both their statements. "I think it's a trap, but I'm not sure how. Keep your head on a swivel and stay close. Raph, I don't know where we're going."

He slid to the left to step in front of me, but I stopped him with my arm.

He removed it. "The safest way is for me to lead. Put Chloe between us."

I stepped behind Chloe. I hated not being in front, but he was right. I took a deep breath and blew it out slowly, willing my pounding heart to slow down. With my brush still in hand, I whispered, "Go."

CHAPTER FOURTEEN

We left the shuttle, and time both sped up and slowed down. Everything was happening too fast while I moved in slow motion. My heart pounded in my ears as we stuck to the side of the shuttle before moving across the yard toward an opening in a wall. There were a few people moving about who only gave us a cursory glance. They were all Cerulean, but none of them seemed surprised to see us.

The oppressive heat hit me in the face like a slap from a steaming blanket. It had a physical weight to it that pressed me into the ground. Breathing felt like inhaling a sludgy liquid, and my lungs struggled to process it. I had trained on a variety of planets in my years, but this might be the most extreme combination of gravity, humidity, and heat that I had experienced. After so long on assignment, I was out of shape when it came to adapting.

The yard had a half dozen shuttles of similar build to the one we had exited. However, most had fancy paint jobs, a sign that they were used on the planet rather than for exiting the atmosphere, which would strip the paint job. We could travel the stars, but we couldn't develop a neon-pink paint that could survive re-entry.

It didn't appear to be a military yard so much as a parking lot. We passed a particularly expensive shuttle with garish painting and a series of numbers on the side. It appeared to be a business advertisement for a local cake shop.

"Raph, slow down and relax." I stepped up to be in line with him, my hand on Chloe's hand, guiding her between us. "We'll draw more attention by sneaking."

"This doesn't feel right."

"I know." My unease had shifted. I was still suspicious but also deeply confused.

We exited the yard, and I missed a step as the castle became visible in the distance. It was like a scene from a fairy-tale book, the kind that used to grace some countries on Earth, according to the books I had read as a child.

But instead of the grey stone I had seen in pictures, it was a red that matched the dirt ground we strode across. In fact, most of the structures that weren't metal were the same red as the castle and ground. I took a split-second glance up into the air and was able to spot our ship directly overhead, though it was small because of its location beyond the planet's atmosphere. But it did confirm that we were on Cerulea, and we could possibly make it back to my ship within a few hours.

I followed Raph's lead around the wall, and when the stolen law enforcement shuttle was in sight, I didn't sprint, daring to hope we could get there before we were caught. When I leaped up the steps and crossed the threshold, I let out a breath I hadn't realized I was holding. Closing the door, I turned around to start the shuttle and slammed right into Horton.

"Liz! I thought you were deader than a diorite dealer." He squeezed me to his smooth, scaly chest, slightly blubbering in his delivery, before stepping back and shyly adding, "I mean Captain Laika."

I squeezed his arm as I nudged past him to get to the primary control station. "Liz is fine during covert rescue missions. This is hardly the time for standard procedure. Everyone, buckle up. If we can clear the atmosphere, we'll be back at the ship in no time."

People said that most accidents happened within a few kilometers of home, and billions of hours of research, possibly even trillions, hadn't changed a thing. Leaving the atmosphere was still the most dangerous part of any trip. That was why only shuttles could do it, and ships were built in hangars in open space. It was far too dangerous to try to launch a ship from a planet's surface. A lot of good officers and crews had died trying.

But there would be no launch accidents today. Raph was already halfway through the pre-flight checks, his long dark fingers dancing across the surface like a maestro musician. I started my sequence, though I was really only slowing him down.

Chloe was still hyperventilating by the door.

I turned around to spy Horton securing a lumpy square box to an empty chair. "Can you help Chloe sit down and get her to breathe a bit slower?"

I checked on the security protocol installed onboard. It was far superior to anything we had on our ship, which wasn't hard because our ship's features were centuries out of date. But the shuttle had a few tricks that I thought were still only in the testing phase. The scanning range was triple the distance I expected on the 3D display and used a logarithmic scale so a pilot could monitor far and near threats on the same model rather than switching back and forth.

The technology wasn't new, but the training needed to understand it was. Luckily for me, I was a quick learner, though I hoped not to need it at all. I ran through the other options, many of which I had never seen in person.

I had specialized in research vessels, my heart being in discovering the unknown. And after losing both my parents at war, combat could never hold my heart. Fighting would always represent bitter loss rather than noble sacrifice. I was proud that they had saved so many lives, but it was at my family's expense, a fact I could never overcome.

But even a research vessel needed protection against threats, both sentient and environmental, so nothing in the shuttle's arsenal was new to me. But all of it was bigger, badder, and three steps ahead of what I had learned at the academy.

Grappling hooks, collision mitigation safety devices, and explosives of every variety were easy options. It also had the strongest shields and exterior hull I had seen in any shuttle, let alone one that could reach the speeds it showed on its specs. "Dang."

Raph nodded, his fingers not slowing their dance across the instrument panel. "I know. Can we keep it?"

"We'll be lucky to keep our skins and our jobs."

"Maybe we should just jet off to a faraway planet and start life anew?"

I didn't reply, letting the idea sit in my brain for a bit. I wouldn't ever seriously consider that. *Would I?*

The engines began to roar, the sound rising above the gentle hum it had produced at standby.

"Raph, I'm going to keep an eye out if you want to take the lead." We were both capable of running the shuttle solo, as he had done when they flew down.

I was still awed by that. They had broken every imaginable rule, stolen a law enforcement shuttle, and gone on a rogue rescue mission. *For me.* The pressure in my chest increased until tears were pressing against my eyelids, itching to fall down my face. It was only the adrenaline thundering through my veins that kept me from breaking down in gratitude, along with decades of training, the fact that we were still in unknown amounts of danger, and maybe more than a hint of vanity.

My brain had taken it upon itself to tear into a million pieces and try to have every possible thought at once. I thought of all the things that could have happened or could still happen, and the murder that turned into murders and why. I weighed all the possible paths ahead of us, forking again and again at every decision we made. Even my rescue could be an elaborate trap meant to crush me in its gaping maw.

No. I needed to trust in something, and that was my crew. This crew specifically. The three crew members with me had been there since day one, and in every one of those days, they had shown evidence of their character. I never made the conscious decision to trust them, but if it was required, then now was the moment. I trusted them with my life in the most literal sense. If they were going to betray me, I would fall for it. Some things were worth believing in.

"I trust you," I said out loud, startling myself.

"You'd better because I am about to save all our butts," Raph said before taking off with such force that I heard Chloe and Horton hit the floor with an oomph.

"Buckle up as best you can. Raph, try to fly casually. We don't want to draw unnecessary attention."

"We'll be out of here so fast they won't even—uh-oh."

Lights flashed on the panel, and I ran through all the sequences to check. "At least two shuttles are in position behind us. I think they're going to—"

I was cut off when a mild eruption rocked the shuttle, and the blinking lights were joined by a panicky beeping noise.

Chloe squealed. "What was that?"

"Shut up. I'm trying to focus!" Raph shouted while maneuvering the shuttle at a steep angle to the left then lower, all while accelerating.

I turned around in my seat. Horton and Chloe were holding hands. Neither of them had been through the same training Raph and I had received, which included combat evasive tactics and counter-maneuvers.

"It'll be okay. Raph and I are the best in the fleet, and no one is going to get the better of us." I took a moment to look each of them in the eye until they nodded.

I turned back to the controls, shocking even myself that what I had said was true. Confidence was a funny creature, coming to me when I least expected it. I fumbled a bit with the new-to-me controls and viewing system. But my training was spectacular, and before I knew it, I was oriented and ready. "Shields are good. Do you want me to port over my view to you?"

Raph had adjusted our flight from perpendicular to the surface of the planet to parallel as we raced above the landscape. "They could hit us if they want."

"They don't want to. Try circling hard twenty degrees on the plane of orientation."

Straight ahead was both zero degrees and three hundred sixty degrees with one eighty directly behind. Using the orientation of the shuttle and the pilots, the degree went around clockwise, like a traditional Earth compass. Anything more complicated would be explained with computer coordinates. Only in a dog fight would we skip all that. Basically, I asked him to turn a little to the right.

He nodded and adjusted our travel direction. He jerked back a moment later as the right side of the panel lit up. A second later, the window illuminated with a missed shot.

"Try three-forty degree." Asking him to turn left, I pulled up an overhead map of the overall terrain.

Down below, the red planet slid by, giving me only the briefest glimpses of houses, cities, and pockets of civilization.

As soon as we banked left, Raph jerked us back to the right with another near miss. "We have more company overhead."

I checked, and sure enough, four more shuttles had joined the fight. They were flying above us. Raph jerked the shuttle down toward the planet, but still we were thrown around when multiple shots impacted the top of the craft.

Chloe screamed, and Horton let out a sickly moan.

But I barely noticed and didn't have time to comfort them as a cold sweat broke across my chest and face. "Raph?"

"I can't go any faster." He took us lower. Mountains loomed on either side of us, giving us shelter. "Do we have any way to fire back?"

"Nothing that would do more than inconvenience them and not enough to take on all six. We're set up for defense rather than offense. Do what you can."

I checked over the map and saw we were rapidly approaching a large body of water, an ocean from the size of it, if that classification was accurate on Cerulea. I had no time to worry about the taxonomy of bodies of water because we were hit from overhead again.

Our shields were taking a beating but holding up as Raph dropped lower. Arches and swooping valleys passed under us. It would have been gorgeous if not for the fact that we were racing away in a bid to save our lives.

The shuttle rocked back and forth and up and down as Raph did some of the best flying I had ever seen or experienced. His piloting was smooth, and he adjusted quickly. Any single false move, and we would be nothing more than a smear and shrapnel on the red rocks below. We had to slow down significantly, but so did the shuttles chasing us. In fact, they slowed down so much that I started to believe we could lose them.

Finally, after an eternity of racing across the landscape, we shot out over the blue waters. The ships behind us pulled off hard to the side, moving along the coastline. I realized that we hadn't been chased. We had been herded. But for what purpose?

I looked down at the water and noticed a particularly dark patch moving to the surface. I barely had time to open my mouth and shout, "Pull up!" before the creature breached the surface, its mouth open.

I slammed my hand on a button on the panel. And we

were enveloped in darkness.

CHAPTER FIFTEEN

The crash was tremendous. Every safety device in the shuttle went off at once, causing blindness and deafness that still somehow managed to overwhelm every single sensation I had. Then the long, aching sensation of falling led to a second, only slightly softer, stop.

I couldn't tell which way gravity was pulling me. My back and neck felt like a giant hand had reached under my skin and squeezed and stretched every muscle beyond its length then squished it back. My head was ringing, and every square inch of my skin burned, probably from the explosives released at impact to slow the momentum of the ship. Without it and the thousands of other safety features in the shuttle, we would have been smashed like bugs on a windshield.

The view through the front window was pitch-black. The impact had knocked out all the lighting except the emergency red lights. My hands had a few smears of black on them that I realized was blood from where my arms had hit something. I accessed the accident-evaluation table.

I attempted to crane my neck to look around but immediately regretted the motion. My hand flew up to my neck before I could stop it. Whiplash had definitely occurred, and my shoulder wasn't doing too hot, either, from where the safety harass had dug into me.

The first and most important evaluation flashed on the screen. Four persons were identified, and their vitals were at high stress levels, but no one was in immediate danger.

I closed my eyes in relief. "Thank you, Lord," I whispered, my voice tight and caught in my throat. By no means did that mean our troubles were over, but at least we had made it this far. A lump formed in my throat. Things had gotten serious in a way I hadn't been able to contemplate thus far.

When I was kidnapped in the shuttle, I had worried about myself. But there was something different about being responsible for someone else. Theoretically, that had always been the case. As captain of my ship, I had my crew under my protection, but that had never really been an issue when going back and forth to deliver mail and the occasional passenger.

Suddenly, and in a way I never expected, reality was setting in and, with it, a raising panic. I couldn't deal with it now, or ever if I had my choice. The literal pain in my neck felt as though the very weight of my head was too much to hold, which was distraction enough to allow me to ignore the rising panic attack.

The ship shifted suddenly then jerked twice. A yelp of pain and several groans from my crew set my priorities. I ran my hand across the panel in front of me, stabilizing gravity and locking in the recovery system routine. I scanned the report and let out a sigh of relief that things weren't worse. Someone out there deserved a medal for whatever programming had been installed for collision mitigation because it had worked like a champ.

Gravity was restored, giving the sensation that the ship was righted though the monitors showed otherwise.

I unlocked my harness and turned to Raph. Placing a hand on his shoulder I gently squeezed. "Raph, are you okay?"

He winced, and his eyes fluttered open. "Where are we? What happened?"

"I'll get to that in a second." I moved back to Horton and Chloe.

Chloe had pinky-orange blood crawling down her face, lighter colored than my own. She was talking gently to Horton and pulling on his hand. "He's not waking up." Her voice carried a hint of distress.

"Horton?" I stepped around him and grabbed the medical assessment unit off the wall. I pressed it to the center of his chest.

As the machine's lights flickered to indicate its progress, he spoke. "I'm fine."

"Can you open your eyes?"

He twisted his head. The skin cracked as it folded, blackened bits still clinging in the creases. "Just let me…" He paused, sucked in air hard, and let out a groan. "I think I crushed something, but it will be—"

He breathed in hard again, making the entire shape of his chest change. He grunted, and I heard a faint snap. When he exhaled, his chest held the shape, and I realized he had reset a crushed chest. He was far tougher than I had ever guessed.

The lights that had been flickering red and yellow turned solid red then transitioned to green. The beeping took a less urgent tone.

Chloe unbuckled and stepped over the deflated pressure bags that had exploded on impact. She extended her hand. "Let me have that." She was covered in pink impact patches, but overall, she appeared to move a lot better than I felt.

I passed her the medical assessment unit. She ran it over Horton and pressed on the panel, her eyebrows knitted.

He twisted in his seat. "Where is my bag?"

Loose items during impact were one of the greatest risks, so they were usually locked down. But research had shown that passengers, even those with fleet training at the highest levels, had items out during transit. Even a small tablet or work unit could become a deadly projectile.

I searched the back of the ship and found the roughly square package stuck in a corner. Using a combination of gravity specific sensors, the bundle had been directed to an empty corner before its speed had been decelerated before impact. I picked it up, and much like the rest of us, it seemed only slightly damaged.

When I handed it to Horton, he clutched it to his chest and ran a hand over each angle with such intensity that I was concerned that the crash had left him with a head injury and confusion.

Chloe stood up, her assessment over. "Horton had been hurt badly. Dislocated tail. Most of his core is popped out of place in one way or another. Many broken ribs. The seats just…" She snorted air out through her gills and turned away.

I shared her anger. Ignesians, despite serving in the fleet for years, still suffered from a lack of support. They were too tall and their bodies too differently shaped from humanoids to really function well on ships and shuttles. The fleet said they were happy for anyone to serve, but it was just lip service.

"It's just a crick," said Horton. "I'll be good as new before you can whistle twice." He pushed up out of the seat. His tail unnaturally twisted to the left, he moved slowly but with great effort, grunting with each step. "Where are we? What happened?"

Raph was still seated but unbuckled, so he could turn enough to face us. He held his hands out in the air in front of him unnaturally, as if he were about to type on an imaginary keyboard. "I didn't crash." It was a statement but also a bit of defense.

I shook my head at the unspoken implication. "No. Something hit us. From out in the water."

"Oh!" Chloe said, realization in her voice. "A gulper."

"What's that?" Raph snapped back.

"They are like a fish but breathe air. I'm not sure of the UL word. They can eat metal. There was an episode a few seasons ago that showed them recycling metal from other worlds. There is a big fireworks display, and they shoot the metal out over the water. When the gulpers die, their bodies wash up on shore, and the king harvests them. The bones are mostly made of the metal they eat, and it is this amazing shimmery color. It's super expensive. They fashion it into jewelry and other ornate objects to export. No one flies over the water for that reason."

"Why didn't you say something?" Raph shouted.

"I couldn't see where we were from back here, and everything was happening so fast. Don't you have some sensors you should have been checking?"

"Stop!" I shouted at both of them. "We do not point fingers at anyone but the people trying to kill us. Got it?"

Raph winced and turned his head away, his arms still stiff in front of him.

"Chloe, run a health check on Raph. I'm concerned about navigator breaks." It was a common name for injuries sustained by navigators on impact. Because they always had their arms on the panel, even during an impact, they often experienced fractures to the ulna and radius bones.

"I'm fine," Raph said but with no conviction, probably more a prayer for it to be true rather than a genuine belief that it was.

Chloe looked at his arms and made an unhappy noise as she ran a diagnosis unit over them. When she finished, she gently lowered them onto the armrests of his chair. "Captain, where's the first-aid kit?"

"I'll get it," I said and hurried to retrieve it.

I had a general idea of where they were usually kept and why she should stay focused on Raph. She was being calm, but his unusually testy manner made me believe it was worse than she let on.

"Is there anything more you know about the gulper?" I called out to her.

"Not really. They talk a lot about the material but not the animal. It is really special because it has the soft organic feel of a natural material but the brilliant coloring of a gem. They say it is like an Earth gem called an *opal*." She said it with an odd emphasis. "It has flashes of red and green, sometimes even blue or purple. It can be shaped a little but not like metal. They say it feels wonderful and has mystic powers, though that may just be clever branding. This is the only place in the known universe where it is created. The king is in charge of all of it and only allows a little to be sold at a set price. He got the idea from studying how ancient Earth handled diamonds. Did you know that they used to cost so much money that people saved up for years to give their beloved a ring with one?"

"None of this is useful," Raph said through clenched teeth.

I put down the box of supplies and dug out an injection unit to pass to Chloe. She entered a sequence and pressed the unit into the bicep of each of his arms. Each press made a small whooshing noise.

The tension in Raph's face eased, and he closed his eyes with a small sigh. "Thank you."

Chloe turned to me. "That's most of what I know. They are always borrowing jewelry for big events and bragging about it. Like advertising or something. It is their biggest export after reality shows, but it's all intermeshed. I tried to look up the pricing on a bracelet, and it was a year's wages."

"But the locals can buy it?"

"No. Technically, no one on Cerulea owns any of the material. It all goes to the king to export, though he sometimes loans it out. I need you to help me with this." She had unpacked a thin plastic mesh. "I need to set some supports on his arms for the next twenty-four hours. The fractures aren't bad, but I need to do this correctly, so they heal properly."

I nodded and stepped up to be her assistant. She moved my hands into place, and I held his fingers and elbow at the exact angle she instructed.

Raph kept his eyes closed, and his skin was cold and clammy. His only reaction was the barest of movements at the corner of his mouth as Chloe worked. The mesh would allow air through and was washable while still being light and strong.

Using a portable UV light, she set the material that would stay stiff until cut off. Within fifteen minutes, we were done, and Raph, still under the effects of the painkiller, was more relaxed. Chloe set two bone-growth-acceleration nodes over each end of the fracture and activated them, which would help cut the healing time exponentially.

With an additional follow-up check on the rest of us, Chloe gave her final verdict. "We are in pretty good shape. It could have been much, much worse."

An alarm flashed on the panel as a warning blared.

Raph took a quick look. "Shields are at fifty percent. Extreme corrosive agents detected on one hundred percent of the exterior surface. Exterior breach expected in twenty minutes."

It *was* much worse. We were about to be liquidated.

CHAPTER SIXTEEN

"What's happening?" Horton shouted as he clung to Chloe's arm. In spite of his large size and impressive physique, he acted like a small child clinging to his mother for comfort.

I wouldn't have minded doing the same, but I was in charge and the only one who really had all the information. "We are inside a large aquatic animal that can digest metal. I noticed the way the pursuing ships hung back at the coast, and I had a split second to see the creature breach the surface. I activated the grappling hooks, and it appears..."

I ran my fingers over the panel, but nothing in its programming prepared it for diagramming whale anatomy. "Well, we are somewhere inside it. If it digests metal, it's going to eat right through the hull, compromise the ship's integrity, then digest us." That wasn't exactly how I preferred my final moments to occur. I had thought we were going to have a lot more time to come up with a solution. "Chloe, do you know anything more from your shows?"

"Not really. Can't we do a data search?"

I shook my head and glanced around. "The reception is

lousy in here."

Chloe giggled, eyes dancing. "Can't we, like, blow it up?"

Raph was at the panel, working on the screen. "We don't have much firepower, but I can try. Everyone buckle up as best you can. Chloe, Horton, pick different seats."

"But I want to be able to see," said Chloe.

"And I don't want you to die," Raph fired back.

I did my best to anchor myself into my chair. "New seats have unfired airbags."

"Oh," said Chloe, sobering quickly. "What about you and Raph?"

"We have no choice. It is what it is. Now, let us focus, and if you want to help, pray."

I pulled up the scan I had run onto the area, though it was about what I figured. We were anchored by the grappling equipment to something fleshy shaped in what was essentially a long tube. I was going to guess the throat, where digestion enzymes existed but probably weren't as strong as the main stomach area of the creature. We might have had more time if we hadn't been hit so many times by the pursuing shuttles.

Raph lowered his voice. "I'm not sure that we could fire our way out of a paper bag, let alone this meat suit we are trapped in. Nothing here is going to do much more than tickle a creature this big."

"Tickle, eh?" I patted the book at my thigh. "I think that will be perfect. Hold on back there. I have an idea, and if it works, things are going to get pretty violent."

"What's up, Cap?"

"Everyone locked in?" I shouted.

Once everyone answered in the affirmative, I lowered the gravity in the ship. We shifted to the left and slightly forward as the planet's gravity took over. Then, as I suspected, the ship rolled for a few seconds, then a quick couple of shakes left and right happened before the vibrating occurred again.

"I'm going to be sick," moaned Horton.

"You're not the only one, and that might be exactly what saves us," I said over my shoulder before turning to Raph. "You ever had something stuck in your throat like a pill or bit of food? You try to swallow and maybe shake your head. That is what the animal is doing."

"Can't it cough us up?"

"Not if it has a blow hole. The respiration system is probably not connected to its digestion. Anyway, animals like that only have one way to clear their throat if something is stuck and bothering them."

Raph's eyes lit up. "I get it. So we are going to wait until it throws us up then fly out lickety-split?"

"Right idea, but I don't think we can risk waiting around. Let's irritate its throat a bit more." My hand hovered over the arsenal panel.

The swinging motion increased.

"Oh yeah, now you're talking." Raph adjusted his seat to get closer to the panel and winced at the movement. "Release the grappling hooks. I can do this."

I glanced at him. "You sure you got this?"

He met my look with a firm nod. "Definitely."

"Hey, guys! After we get vomited up, then what? Like, can this shuttle swim?"

"Water falls within the range of atmospheric conditions that shuttles are built for, but we're going to be at a big disadvantage." I readied the grappling hooks. "Goal one is going to be to get out of the water. Goal two is to land someplace hidden and assess the situation. I want far away from these creatures."

"Can't we just leave the planet?" asked Chloe.

"I'm not going to risk another encounter with whoever was chasing us, given our shield capacity."

Raph didn't look up from his screen. "Cap, I'm ready."

"Fire at will," I said.

Raph fired off a variety of rounds at the surrounding surfaces, spacing the shots for maximum irritation. The throat of the creature spasmed and jerked with each hit. After the last hit, there was a brief silence, then a deep rumble started, rising in volume and pitch. A wall of sticky yellow mucus appeared at the end of the tunnel, approaching rapidly.

"Brace yourself!" I screamed as I released the hooks.

The wave of liquid hit us, and we vibrated so hard my vision doubled. The safety system kicked in, and the movement lessened for a moment before we shot out of the mouth of the creature. We were close to the surface, and I was briefly blinded by the return of natural light.

The engines roared to life, and Horton let out a feral cry that lifted the hairs on the back of my neck. I joined him with an animalistic noise of my own.

Tears of happiness pooled in the corners of my eyes. "Great work!" I shouted as I pulled up the map that the shuttle was creating of the surrounding area. Land was close by. "Seventy-five degrees to the coast."

Raph banked hard. "I'm not getting eaten again."

We saw the deep cave at the base of the cliff at the same time.

I pointed. "Raph—"

"Got it!"

There was some structure at the top of the cliff, but my main concern was the large dark opening at the bottom. I watched the water below, unwilling to fully breathe until we had flown over the glittering red sand and pulled into the sheltering rocks.

"Cut power! I don't want to be seen."

"I've got it handled." Raph ran through the sequence to cloak the ship just as a shuttle flew past and disappeared out over the horizon.

CHAPTER SEVENTEEN

I took a second to start the exterior perimeter evaluation before unbuckling to stand up to face my crew. "Right. We are totally off the books at this point. I don't know who we can trust because someone helped those Ceruleans get me off board. The only ones I trust are the three of you. Chloe, I want you to figure out everything we have onboard: supplies, medical gear, extra clothes, everything. We need to know what we are working with."

Raph turned to the panel. "I can do a system's check. See what shape the ship is in."

"Horton can do that. Take my chair, Raph."

He turned to me in surprise. "My hands are—"

"It's not that. I know that you have some... *ways* of getting information that are not a hundred percent on the up-and-up. Do you think you could use the shuttle to get in touch with the ship without them knowing?"

Realization crossed his face as his hands moved back to the panel. "Yes, I can do that. What do you want to know?"

"Everything." I blew out a long breath. "Any communications between the officers on the ship and fleet headquarters. Any scrap of information you can get on

Cerulea. I do not want to be caught off guard again. Focus on general planet information, anything that might help. See if any of your favors have sent back information yet." I rubbed my forehead where a headache had formed two days ago and never gone away.

"Hey," Raph said.

I turned to look at him. "What?"

"You're doing a good job. We all are. I doubt there is a shipping crew in the universe that could run a better retrieval unit and few explorer crews that would do half as well inside a sea creature. We're kicking butt."

I nodded abruptly, my throat tight. "Thank you, Raph."

Chloe had pulled supplies from the wall cabinets.

I grabbed a couple of waters to pass out to my crew. "Stay hydrated," I told everyone.

While I drank the clear, clean liquid, I checked the secondary screens. There were no living creatures, poisonous liquids, or physical dangers detected for over a thousand yards. Temperatures, humidity, and air conditions were all suitable for human life. I set the oxygen concentrators to active so they would replenish our supply inside the shuttle, then I unsealed the door.

When I stepped out, the heat immediately hit me. It was still bright outside, but the cave overhead shaded me. I found the temperature to be more comfortable than when I had last been outside. How many hours ago was that? It couldn't have been too long ago, though without my work unit, I had lost all sense of time.

I stifled a yawn and wondered when I had last slept. I didn't think being knocked unconscious by a ban counted as restful sleep, but I couldn't justify taking a nap. Although if pushed beyond my limits, I could make a decision that would risk all our lives. We were injured and in enemy territory.

I walked to the edge of the cave, still hidden in the shadows, and looked out toward the ocean as another shuttle patrol flew by. It was way above the top of the cliff, following the coastline. Maybe the flyovers were standard, or maybe they were still looking for us. It was hard to tell.

With the shuttle powered down, the silence was deafening. After a lifetime of living on a ship, I could sense the absence of the comforting hum that meant that everything was okay. It made me subtly uneasy. In its place, I heard waves crashing on a foreign shore from an ocean that had nearly taken us forever into its black depths.

When I attended advanced flight school, most people had assumed I would take the military track like my parents. They were war heroes, and they'd paid the highest possible price for their service. But people forgot I had already paid that price twice over.

I loved and missed them. I'd thought my destiny was to discover new worlds, new life, and new hope. But here I was in a hostile land with a crew to protect and a life-or-death mission. Destiny claimed us no matter what we did.

I slid the small pocket Bible from the side of my thigh and opened it to the middle, searching for the section that had been my father's favorite. I found the passage and said a quick prayer of thanks to the God that had brought us this far. I read the passage out loud, each word as comforting as a song I knew by heart. "To everything there is a season, and a time to every purpose under the heaven: A time to be born, and a time to die; a time to plant, and a time to pluck up that which is planted."

There was a noise behind me, and I closed the book and slid it into my pocket. I ad-libbed a few lines of my own. "A time to see a murder, and a time to be accused of murder; a time to be kidnapped, and a time to be rescued; a time to be swallowed by a large sea creature, and a time to be vomited up together."

Raph exited the shuttle with Chloe and Horton behind him. As he strode over to me, Chloe and Horton looked around.

Chloe fanned herself. "It's hotter than a basilisk's belly

out here and just as red."

Horton stretched his short arms just barely over his head, his fabric-wrapped box still in one hand. "Feels amazing. Like being next to a volcano during the lava harvests."

"I'm downloading the information you asked for, but the shuttle's evaluation was complete. I think we need to talk." He held out a brown rectangle to me.

For a split second, I thought it was a work unit, though all of ours had been confiscated. "What is this?"

"Let's just say that there was a time I wanted to keep information off my work unit, and it is a good thing because when your ex took all our units, he didn't find this."

It looked just like the fleet-issued work unit except that it was chunkier and heavier and the sides and back were a smooth brown material with darker lines. "Is this wood?"

He nodded. "Makes it undetectable from scans. Ship scanners tend to get easily confused by anything that comes from living organisms, making it a good way to hide technology. Sometimes, the old-fashioned ways are the best."

"So this is how you have been getting all your secret information. Do you guys have one too?"

Horton avoided my eyes.

Chloe squirmed a little. "I would never use it for anything dangerous. I just like my shows."

Over the past few years, since the turnoff from the previous administration, data had been reduced to a need-to-know basis. I struggled to get new books, and if it wasn't for my interest in fleet ship designs, I would run out of things to read halfway through every trip. I couldn't blame any of them. "Okay."

I could almost feel them sigh with relief, though I was a little insulted that they thought I would pick a fight over something so stupid while we were trying to stay alive. I was also a little annoyed that no one thought I might want one of the fake units.

"What did you find out?" I asked Raph.

"The officers had sent a message to fleet headquarters, asking for additional assistance, but they did not update them on anything that happened. The original backup was responsible for escorting the crew back to base. The ship appears to be unmanned right now with no one still on board. I'm also downloading everything I can about Cerulea, focusing on the environment and political situation. The original searches I started when we were onboard were halted, so I restarted them. Plus I relayed a message to some friends that specialize in… unconventional trading to see if they know anything about Cerulea that might be useful."

"Smart. Chloe, what did you find?"

"Lots of supplies but mostly for short-term emergencies. Water, food, and basic survival supplies for a day or two. Some emergency transponders, but they can only communicate with fleet headquarters. A bag of medical stuff, though we put a reasonable dent in it. We have enough basic painkillers for a few more days."

"That should be enough. Horton, can the shuttle get us back to the ship?"

He juggled the square package in his arms to use another of the knockoff work units. "The shields are in rough shape. The grappling hooks caught on something as we exited the creature. Looks like part of a tooth?" He gestured toward the shuttle.

The thing he had referred to was thin and as long as my forearm. It was dark green, but when I moved closer, I could see the color shift subtly from a bright spring green to a deep emerald to a shade that bordered on blue. It came to a point that wasn't terribly sharp until one considered the force that would have been exerted by the terrible jaw where it had resided. The leading edge was sharp enough to put a thin nick in my fingertip when I ran it down the length. The bottom was broken like a snapped branch, the color seeping all the way through the tooth rather than just a surface feature.

"It's gorgeous. If this is how the whole skeletal structure is, I can see why it is so valuable. It was caught on the grappling hook? Didn't it retract when it was released?"

"Whatever gunk that thing had in its throat had already eaten most of the way through the mechanism. Somewhere along the way, the opening caught the tip of the tooth and snapped it off. Unfortunately, that same stomach acid got into the opening, and it is slowly eating its way into the ship. It will be compromised within twelve hours."

I opened my mouth to ask a question, but he continued.

"The orbit of the planet is such that our ship is moving farther from our location. See?" He pointed out over the ocean. "Near the left edge of the cave about thirty degrees above the horizon, there is our ship. The spin of the planet is such that the distance is going to increase. If we leave right now, it will take us ten hours to arrive."

"How sure are you on all these numbers?"

"I am quite literally betting the whole lava farm on it." Horton turned the screen to show me a field of numbers that meant nothing to me.

"And the shield will hold through exiting the atmosphere?" I asked.

"Once."

I blew out a breath through my teeth. "That is about the worst possible news we could get that still qualifies as good news."

Chloe gave me a small smile while Raph chuckled. Horton made a noise like a coughing hiccup that I took to be agreement.

"Here's the plan. We have a tight timeline, but I don't want to make a mistake. Chloe, I want you to do another quick health check on everyone as we prepare the ship. We will aim to get into the air within thirty minutes, where we will make a straight shot to the ship. It is still incapacitated, but we can use the lockdown room while I send a formal notification to my representative that—what is that noise?"

There was an urgent beeping that was unfamiliar to me. Raph raised his unit then flipped around to stare out of the cave. I followed his line of sight just in time to see our freighter ship, which was in orbit around the planet, explode. Even as far from us as possible, the intensity of the explosions burned the image into my retinas. My shock was closely followed by the realization that our one hope of escape had just been vaporized.

My only sense of relief came from knowing that no one was still on the ship.

Horton shoved me aside as he barreled toward the cave entrance. He dropped to his knees, and the package he had been carrying fell to the ground. The blanket slid off to reveal that he had been carrying a wooden box with a red light on the side.

Before I had time to puzzle out that mystery, he howled in an anguished scream that was so low and deep that it vibrated in my gut. "No! Eugene!"

Chloe raced to his side to hold him, but I was rooted in place. Our last chance of escape was gone, and we were marooned on a hostile planet. But I still felt that his extreme grief was uncharacteristic for anyone, let alone him, a being who had thus far weathered every adversity well.

The box at his side lit up, and a mechanical voice spoke. "It's okay, Tonny. I'm here."

Horton ceased wailing and slowly turned to the box. He lifted it to eye level. "Eugene?"

"What in the name of photons is going on?" Raph asked.

"Not a flipping clue," I replied, sure that my inevitable mental break had finally occurred.

CHAPTER EIGHTEEN

Horton hugged the box to his chest, stroking it with his thick fingers, the talons dragging across the wooden surface. "How? When? I told you that you couldn't come!" He turned the box so the light faced him.

The mechanical voice returned, the red light flashing with each syllable. "I wanted to come along and experience the planet. Plus what if you needed me? I wanted to help save the captain too."

"You got to listen—oh never mind. Eugene, I'm just glad that you're okay." Horton hugged the box to his chest and turned his large head to rest it on the surface.

"Did I have a stroke?" I asked.

"Nah, Cap. I'm seeing it too."

"Our ship blew up!" Chloe said in an empty tone as she sat next to Horton in the red dirt.

I patted her shoulder. "I know, but I think I need to sort this out first. Horton, please explain."

Horton rocked the box in his arms, his eyes closed.

"Horton!"

Horton jerked his head up and looked around. He slowly returned from wherever he had been mentally. He cleared his throat and stood up. "Captain Laika, this is

Eugene."

"I thought you said Eugene was just a pet name for the engine, but I suppose it is safe to assume there was more to that story?"

Horton twisted his foot on the ground. "Yes, I had never been away from home for so long, and it's really lonely in the engine room, so I installed a little artificial intelligence program to keep me company."

Raph stomped over. "You installed an AI on my ship? Those are banned for a reason! How dare you?"

"They aren't so bad, and I was really careful. The parameters were pretty strict. At least at first."

Raph jabbed a finger at the box. "That's what they said before, but look at what happened at Gamma X. An AI highjacked the whole ship for two weeks."

"They were attempting to take kids to a slave planet for punishment because of petty offenses!" Horton countered, his voice rising in anger.

"The whole crew was locked out of control."

"Because the captain was a bad man. The AI was right."

"And what if that thing decided *we* were wrong and cut us off?"

The red light on the box was flashing in an agitated pattern. "I would never do that. You're a good crew. Captain Laika is the best captain around despite what the official records at fleet administration say."

Horton took a step toward Raph. "You were plenty happy to take the bonuses we got when Eugene tweaked the engine."

"Eugene," I interrupted, "what does it mean that you are here rather than on the ship?"

Everyone stopped talking to look at me then at the box in Horton's arms.

"Eugene, answer me!"

"Yes, Captain Laika," its tinny voice replied. "This wooden box is where I store my programming during docking when fleet runs a virus-detection program. We actually have a few spares in case one is damaged. When Horton said he was going on a rescue mission, I convinced him to take a spare with him to gather data so I could process it when he returned."

Chloe smiled at the box. "Aw, you were bringing your program back a toy."

I shushed her and gestured for the box to continue. "And you stowed away?"

The red light flashed twice. "Yes, I copied over my main program, along with my database of previous decisions. Tonny relies on me, and I knew I might be of help."

"Tonny?"

"I took the last syllable of his name and added the Y because my research indicates that it is common for entities that spend a considerable amount of time together through work or by choice to give each other name variations as a sign of affection. He calls me Genie."

I let out a sigh. "And what is the effect of you leaving the ship?"

Eugene did not reply immediately.

I took a gamble based on the interaction we had so far. "Eugene, you need to tell me the truth." I didn't have any experience with AIs since the fleet outlawed them ten years before I was born, and I had always lived on a fleet vessel when not in fleet training. But I did have experience as a captain working with crew members, and I could lean into that. "Genie, I'm the captain, and I'm in charge here. You know that I need an honest answer."

Eugene made a noise that sounded like a sigh. "I had to decide where my main programming and decision database would go. I can be in multiple places at once if the programming can communicate and integrate the information in real time, but this unit doesn't have the ability to communicate with the ship beyond a kilometer unless I have access to a larger communications portal. I left a perfectly adequate replica behind. It should have been able to keep the ship stable without my presence. But you do realize that the ship would have exploded long ago without me, right?"

"Uh… pardon?"

"The ship had a virus. Horton and I were the only reason it ran. It should have exploded within the first few months."

My ship? I turned to Horton, unable to form words in my shock.

Horton rubbed his foot in the dirt and avoided my eyes. "Fleet wouldn't do anything. We had it under control."

I finally stammered out a question. "How do you know that?"

"I reported it, and they claimed it didn't show in any of their scans. Even when I tried to show them, they said I was just making a mistake. I removed it with Eugene's help, but six months later, it showed up again, right after we docked. I'm sorry, Captain. I wasn't sure if you'd believe me."

I paused, waiting for some emotion to assault me, but nothing came. Eventually, it was clear that the numbness I felt *was* my reaction. I could have questioned the little AI's assertion, but in my core, it felt true.

Raph had a tumultuous history with the fleet, but he wasn't willing to easily accept that they were so faulty that they couldn't locate a virus. "We don't know if that box is telling the truth. It probably messed up the ship. It wasn't supposed to be installed at all, and now our ship has blown up. We have to wipe its memory before fleet finds us."

Horton tore over to Raph, towering over him by at least a foot and outweighing him by probably more than a hundred scaly pounds of pure muscle. "Don't you blame Eugene! That ship has been a death trap since day one, and I couldn't have kept it from blowing up without Genie's help. I tried to get help from fleet, and they either gave me the runaround or ignored me. Plus, someone dumped a gosh-darned toolbox full of tools into the engine, or did you forget that part?"

I had never seen Horton angry, let alone as angry as he was now. The air vibrated with his voice.

Raph stepped back, his mouth moving like a fish out of water.

Horton advanced, the box under one arm and the other hand jabbing a talon at Raph. "If you wipe Eugene's database, that would wipe his memory. Even if I reinstalled it, he wouldn't be the same program. You can't kill Genie!"

The little red light flashed quickly. "Navigator Raphael, often, my programming assisted you during your course corrections to help you be a better pilot."

Raph stepped back as though he had been slapped, then rage contorted his face. "I don't need help from anyone to fly. I'll wipe you myself."

I stepped between them, pushing Horton back. Fortunately, he gave in freely to my pressure. "Enough. Nobody is wiping anyone. But Horton, you need to promise not to ever install Genie anywhere else without my permission."

Horton nodded.

I waited then addressed the wooden box. "Genie, I need you to promise as well and code that into your programming."

The red light flashed. "But what if you are unconscious and can't give permission? What if I have data gathered that you don't know about? What if your life is at risk?"

I rubbed my forehead. I should have taken those philosophy electives. "What can you promise?"

The little red light turned on and off in a pattern for five or six seconds. "All my programming and databases are consistent with the idea that you are a good captain, and if I was on your crew, then I would adhere to the guidelines you set because you have demonstrated that you care for your ship and crew in a way that my findings determine will be beneficial to long-term survival."

For a machine, he had a way with words. I smiled at him. "That is probably the nicest thing a machine has ever said to me. Horton, I need your verbal agreement as well. I don't want to be caught off guard again."

"Yes, Captain."

Chloe was watching the entire interaction from a distance, but Raph was still fuming, his nostrils flaring with each breath.

"Raph?" I asked.

He looked at me, his mouth twitching like he wanted to say something but his brain was holding it back.

I gestured at the sky beyond the cave, where our last hope of escape had recently exploded. "We need to get over this and anything else because we need to work together or we'll all die." Dying was pretty high on the list of possibilities whether we got along or not, but it didn't seem like the right time to share that news. The tension in the group was as high as the heat and humidity.

The little red light flashed. "Navigator Raphael, based on a reply you made, I believe I haven't given you enough context to understand the intention behind my comment. I have assisted you when you controlled the ship. But based on my analysis of your control movements compared to the research Horton downloaded for me of other fleet navigators, you are approximately thirty-four percent more efficient than the rest of the fleet. I have not found another navigator that exceeds you in efficient movement control, reaction time, or decisions made that resulted in a positive net gain."

Raph's eyebrows shot up. "Are you saying that I am the best navigator in the whole fleet?"

"I have not evaluated every single navigator, but based on the ones I have evaluated, it is unlikely that there is a superior navigator in the fleet. While my assistance improved your performance, you are already far superior to any of your peers or higher-ranked officers."

Raph's mouth opened and closed very slowly. Then he nodded. "Okay, I accept your apology."

Chloe took a drink from a purple bottle. "That's just great. Now we can all hold hands and sing while we wait for certain death." She hiccuped then blew out a raspberry.

I snatched the bottle from her hand. "What is this?"

She giggled. "Medicine."

I gave it a good sniff then pulled my head back and blinked hard to clear my eyes. "It's mostly alcohol. Go drink some water and sober up because we are going to need everyone to make this plan work."

"How?" Chloe stumbled slightly to the side. "I heard the report. We can't use the shuttle to do *anything*. We're just going to die on this forsaken red oven!"

I grabbed her shoulders and turned her to face me. "We can still use the shuttle for something. Misdirection." I turned to Raph, Horton, and my newest official crew member, Eugene. "Let's go into the shuttle, and I'll explain."

CHAPTER NINETEEN

Within the hour, the plan was ready. For better or for worse, we were committed. Chloe had been monitoring the cave entrance. She confirmed that every fourteen minutes, a shuttle passed overhead cruising down the coastline from the left. They would then disappear off to the right as the cliffs blocked her view.

Our stolen police shuttle was in pretty bad shape. We moved it onto the beach exactly thirteen minutes after a patrol had passed. The shuttle slowly, and quite unsteadily, rose until it was roughly level with the top of the cliff. Raph held the shuttle there for fifteen seconds until the next patrol appeared around the bend, right on schedule.

Eugene's red light flashed with excitement. "The patrol has locked on with their scanner. Go!"

Our shuttle shot toward the atmosphere in what we hoped looked like a frantic bid for escape, but the patrol shuttle was right its tail. They must have switched out shuttles from the ones that had chased us earlier in the day because this one had massive firepower.

The first shot missed, but the second and third were direct hits. The police shuttle abruptly shifted directions with each hit, and part of the ship fell off into the ocean below, causing the gulpers to rise to the surface. Finally, as we had suspected would be the case, the patrol shot a rocket. It rose into the air, slowly gaining on our former transport until the moment of impact. The resulting explosion was so bright it looked like a second star had been born in the atmosphere. It probably blinded everyone within miles.

By the time the visual flare had died, there was nothing left in the sky but a faint puff of smoke. The pieces, no bigger than the large red grains on the beach, fell slowly. They looked like a dark cloud slowly drifting down over the ocean.

Raph stood next to me at the entrance of the cave. "Do you think they bought it?"

"I'm hoping so. It is well known that you can't fly a shuttle without being *in* the shuttle. If they believe we were making a mad dash for escape and were killed in the process, they will stop looking for me, or rather us, as they surely knew that someone helped me. Eugene, are you picking up anything?"

A second then a third patrol ship showed up overhead. They hovered at the top of the cliff, oriented toward the ocean.

"Yes," Eugene said. "The first contact patrol is reporting that he picked up the heat signature of four passengers and they refused to listen to his commands to land and be boarded. The pilot says that criminal vessel sent a confusing message in reply, so he followed orders to shoot it down. No survivors."

I looked at the AI suspiciously. "What message did you send?"

"'*Hasta la vista*, baby.' I pulled it from my ancient history database. The context was goodbye because we are leaving in a glorious fashion."

I suppressed a smile. "Well, it worked. In fact, I'm a little concerned with how quickly the three of you rigged that up. Theoretically, the safety programming should have made it impossible for Raph to control a shuttle remotely or falsify passenger heat signatures."

Eugene blinked. "It was Raph. The shuttle was fighting the information being fed to it, but he was able to react faster than it could adjust. No one else could have done it."

Raph's whole face lit up, and he gently tapped his fist on the side of the box. "That's right, Genie. We make a great team."

I narrowed my eyes at the little box. I needed to have a serious discussion with Horton about what abilities the AI had for embellishment. It was good that Raph was no longer angry, but I was concerned about the amount of truth bending that might be going into that endeavor.

"What now?" Chloe called out. She was reclining in a chair we had stripped from the shuttle. Next to her was a pile of everything that hadn't been nailed down. She was holding her bottle but not drinking from it.

We had overridden most of the safety features on the spacecraft except one. All fleet ships had a black box that would send out a signal to headquarters. It had probably first gone off when we were shot at repeatedly, then again after the gulper attack, but most definitely when the shuttle had been vaporized.

I turned back to Chloe. "We wait. We have enough supplies at this point to last a few days in this cave. The fleet was already sending reinforcements, which should be here in the next few hours."

Chloe took a swish from an orange medicine bottle and burped loudly. "But can we trust them? Between framing you and missing a virus that was going blow up our home for the past few years, they are worse than the Ceruleans."

"Let's all sit and talk." I gathered some water that the water recycler had cleaned and passed it around while directing everyone to their chairs. We hadn't had much time to talk, and while I was sure everyone shared Chloe's concerns, they hadn't pressed me for details.

"Drink up. You won't realize how much moisture you are losing in this heat until you get sick." I took a long sip from the container and winced. The water tasted slightly metallic and stale. I knew it was clean, but tasty, it was not.

"The cave goes back only a hundred yards, and except for a hole at the back near the ceiling, there is nothing else in here. There are some footprints smaller than my thumb in a few spots, but otherwise, it has apparently been empty for a long time. A black-box signal requires a thorough investigation, so the fleet will arrive soon. We will rest here until we can get a signal to fleet. Can you do that, Eugene?"

"Affirmative. I'll prepare my signal and set up an automatic scan for when one of their vessels comes within range." His red light flashed slowly with a slight increase in the whooshing sound of his fan.

"We have to trust that whoever is setting me up didn't plan on us having direct contact with fleet. A conspiracy only works when only a few people know about it, and whoever is sent as reinforcements will be following standard protocol. I believe that if we can make contact, they will take us into custody, and things will get worked out." I didn't actually know if that was true, but none of our options were great. I tried to muster an air of confidence that would inspire my crew.

They gave me wary looks that made me think that they could see through my act but had decided to play along anyway.

"What if Officer Ex and his purple-haired sidekick find us first? Surely they're behind your setup."

My gut twisted at the question I had been trying to ignore. I stood up and paced around the area. It was one thing to run into my ex-fiancé, someone I had loved and imagined spending the rest of my life with only to discover how poorly he thought of me, but it was a whole new level to be framed by him.

"They need to find us first. Eugene, are you sure they

weren't on the ship when it exploded?"

"I can only analyze the data Tonny's non-authorized work unit relayed to me as my connection cannot go that far. That information indicates that the two officers sent by fleet headquarters used the ship's shuttle to exit prior to the explosion. I did not find any further communications that indicated where the shuttle was headed."

I nodded. "Either they were concerned that the ship was in danger and moved to a safe distance or they came to Cerulean, but either way, it is unlikely that they returned to headquarters, especially not in our ship's shuttle. In that, they might as well be in a rowboat. They are most likely going to show up here eventually. So on that note, Chloe, I want you to monitor the coast for patrols. Take Eugene with you so he can watch and listen for communications or approaching ships. The rest of us will drag all this equipment to the back of the cave and set up a long-term camp."

The next few hours passed slowly in the heat. My body ached from basically everything from the past two days, but I ignored it. I'd been cut, hit, crushed, burned, and bludgeoned. If getting fried like a piece of bacon in the humid hot air was the worst thing to happen to me the rest of our stay, I would count myself lucky.

The interior of the cave was cooler, and we took turns resting. Horton spent some time on the ground, deeply inflating his lungs and popping his bones and joints back into alignment. Raph took frequent breaks to rest his forearms. He didn't say anything, but the expression on his face was growing steadily more pinched.

By the time we were done, the star that illuminated Cerulea had dipped beneath the horizon, and a chill had taken over the air. Our camp at the rear of the cave was cozy and felt safe. We had a small fire, though we used a compacted fuel that was smokeless and released less carbon monoxide than a traditional campfire. It provided light but wasn't so bright that it would attract attention if a patrol came by.

With the sleeping mats set up, the fire providing light and heat, and everything moved into place, I felt as relaxed as I was going to get until I was able to get the situation resolved.

I went to get Chloe and Eugene. She had fallen asleep against the wall of the cave, and when I gently touched her shoulder, she sat up and exposed one cheek covered in tiny indents from her sandstone pillow.

"What? Huh?" She straightened and stood. "I'm sorry."

"No, it's been a long day. I assume you didn't see anything?" I picked up Eugene.

"Not a single thing." She stretched her arms over her head then scrunched her nose in disgust. "Do we have enough water for me to clean up?"

"There are a few hygiene packs. It won't be as convenient as being on the shuttle, but we have everything we need."

"Even a potty?"

I gestured at a canvas tent erected halfway back in the cave. "Like I said, we have everything." I turned around when something white flashed in my peripheral vision, but nothing was there. I had been experiencing that all afternoon, and I was starting to worry about a head injury.

Chloe eyed the flimsy structure of our bathroom. "I guess it's better than nothing."

"Are you kidding? It is way better than nothing. We did survival training in the academy, and that was way worse than this. Given this heat and our injuries, we wouldn't last two days without all this stuff. The convenience of a bathroom or bedrolls is nothing compared to the water recycler, medicine, and food supplies."

She sulked. "I wasn't complaining."

I resisted the urge to sigh. Her training hadn't prepared her for any of this, and she technically hadn't complained, even if the undertone of her comment had been a little snarky. "I was just trying to see the bright side. We have designated this as our pantry, so why don't you... what?"

A funny look crossed her face, then a big smile broke out.

I followed her stare to see a small brown-and-white creature about a dozen feet behind me, creeping up on us.

CHAPTER TWENTY

I jumped back and put a protective arm in front of Chloe, pushing her back as well. After being eaten by a big sea monster, I was suspicious of the whole planet. "What is it?"

Chloe stepped around me. "Don't worry. It's a caline. I saw one on the show."

The creature was focused on me, though its dark eyes darted around before returning to me. It was walking on four thin legs and vaguely reminded me of one of the tiny purse dogs, but it had a long tail that was whipping back and forth like a cat and a full set of whiskers. Its smooth fur was mostly white with a few brown patches.

It sat down on its haunches to watch me, tipping its head to the side. Its large triangular ears swiveled slightly before it jumped up and paced backward as Horton and Raph approached.

Raph was holding the broken tooth from the gulper like a bat ready to swing if the animal attacked. "Is it poisonous?"

Chloe put a hand on his arm above the cast. "No, not dangerous and not poisonous. It's a pet. Very expensive, and you have to have the king's permission. Poor little guy must be lost." She kneeled and spoke in a baby voice. "Who's a good little pocket pet? Who's a good boy?"

I handed Eugene to Horton and kneeled next to Chloe. I gave the caline a good look, noticing the numerous cuts and scabs under its white fur. A particularly long one started on the end of its snout and went across both sides, ending near its incisors, two on each side. "It has sharp teeth."

"Everything does. I guess they could bite, but they really are harmless. In fact, that is the problem. Apparently, they used to be all over the place, then the Ceruleans imported some kind of spider to eat the small gnats that are everywhere."

"What gnats?" I asked as Raph and Horton returned to the meal, having deemed the small creature harmless.

She looked around and shrugged. "Maybe they are only seasonal? Anyway, the spiders went nutso, something about the atmosphere or gravity or something meant that they got really big, and they decided these guys would be an easier meal than a million gnats."

"The spiders must be huge." On a hunch, I turned my back on the creature and walked toward the fire. Sure enough, the little animal followed me, though he stayed several dozen paces away. His skin clung tightly to his small frame, his bones very visible. I had a good guess as to why he had been shadowing me for the past few hours.

Chloe shrugged. "I've never seen the spiders on the show, but I guess they're big. Caline are now extinct in the wild, so only the king breeds them. Ceruleans aren't big on pets, but at least one of the cast members has one. Calines like to sit on shoulders."

I went over to the water and poured some into a bowl. I carefully approached the creature, who backed away. His toes, unlike a dog's, were long, and I could imagine him using them to climb. Perhaps the tails could grip as well, but right now, it was whipping back and forth as I moved closer. The caline crouched, ready to race away, so I put the water down and stepped back, my hands held up to show I meant no harm.

Once I had moved away, the little part-dog-part-cat creature descended on the water. He loudly lapped it up as his tail flicked left and right with delight.

I dug into our supplies and pulled out a pasty cake. It had been created by the fleet through intense research. Its ingredients were deemed safe for ninety-eight percent of all life-forms. They were branded as nutritional cakes, but they were colloquially called pasty cakes because they had the texture and taste of paste.

I stepped next to Chloe, who was still talking. "Are you a little pocket pet? Who's the cutest little pocket pet? You are. Yes, you are."

"Chloe, hasn't the creature suffered enough?" Raph shouted from his place beside the fire.

She stood up and glared at him then turned to me. "You know that when you give an animal food and water, they will follow you anywhere."

"If only it were so easy with humanoids, eh?" I kneeled again. "Hey, little dude. You want some food?"

The creature had finished off the water and was pushing the bowl around on the sandstone floor with a loud *scrush, scrush* noise at each aggressive lick. He didn't look up.

"Hey, Pox!" I said.

His little head shot up as though he recognized his name. He looked at me, then his gaze slid to the food in my hand. Pox raised his little black nose and sniffed the air, whiskers twitching. He took a few steps toward me and let out a whine.

I put a hand on the ground and half crawled a few steps toward him with my other hand extending the pasty cake. Pox extended his head as far as he could, dancing left and right on his four paws.

We went on like that for a few minutes, me reaching a

bit farther and him extending toward me until he finally took the cake from my hand and raced back to the bowl to lie down with the cake between his paws. He took a few bites and then looked up at me. He blinked slowly in what I imagined was a sign of appreciation.

I walked over to the fire and pulled up a box of supplies that doubled as a seat. "Here's the plan. Eugene, can you continue to monitor for incoming fleet communications, or does your programming need you to do other things?"

"Captain Laika, I will continue to monitor, but I have some questions about the small life-form you fed. Will it be joining our group? Can we be certain that it doesn't carry any viruses or that it isn't a trap of some kind?"

Chloe looked up from her rations. "Genie, you better be careful about questioning any new members of the group."

Raph laughed. "Last in, first out."

Eugene's light flashed slowly. "My records, though limited, do not show that the animal could pose any harm, and pets often calm anxieties, lower blood pressure, and provide early warning when danger approaches. Much like myself, I believe that Pox, as you referred to him, will be a good addition to the group."

I patted the top of the little box. "Excellent choice, Genie. Plus, it is starving and thirsty, and we have enough food and water for a month. 'A time to kill, and a time to heal; a time to break down, and a time to build up.'"

"A quote from the Ecclesiastes, a book of the Bible, King James Translation. Chapter three, verse three. Does that hold certain significance to this moment?"

"For me, yes. It's a verse from a section that my parents often quoted. Now is the time for us to heal and rest and perhaps help a small creature that needs it. Soon enough, we will be fighting, possibly for our lives and career with the fleet."

"In that context, the quote makes sense."

I looked at Eugene thoughtfully. I got the uneasy feeling that the statement was more a reflection on what he thought I wanted to hear rather than a true analysis. I wondered again if lying and flattery were a significant part of his programming. That was definitely a topic of investigation before he could be installed anywhere.

"Horton, Raph, Chloe, why don't you go rest for a few hours? I want someone to be awake at all times. I'll take the first shift."

Chloe walked off with a yawn.

Following her, Raph paused next to me to hand me the gulper tooth. "It's all we have for a weapon. Wake me when you need to sleep."

Horton didn't rise, waiting for the others to leave. "Can I sit with you for a bit, Captain?"

"Of course." After laying the tooth on the ground next to me, I turned my attention to the food I had balanced on my knees.

Pox was slowly edging toward me. I grabbed another pasty cake and held it behind me.

The little animal danced left and right, his paws lightly tapping on the sandstone. His fear seemed to be fighting his hunger, but eventually, hunger won out, and he inched closer, his snout extended as far from his body as possible. Finally, he was able to grab the edge of the cake and yank it out of my hand.

This time he only retreated half as far, and I was sure that the gap would close with time. He was cautious, but like me, he had to trust someone to survive. I poured water into a bowl and placed it as far back as I could reach easily without getting up then turned back to the fire.

"Horton, did you want to ask me something?" I knew he must have a million questions, and though I was hesitant to answer, he deserved those answers. I wasn't sure how much of my history my crew knew. They had never asked, and I had never offered, but my trial had been a public spectacle.

I was so wrapped up in my own thoughts that when he did speak my brain struggled to shift with the conversation.

"You know how on the crew manifesto my name is Brucelious H. Basaltic?"

"Uh... yes. But you go by your middle name, Horton," I said.

"The H stands for Horotico. I'm Horton Basaltic."

I stared at him before eventually admitting that I didn't understand. "What do you mean?"

"My oldest brother is Brucelious *Horotico* Basaltic. When he came back from training, my dad died, and Bruce decided he wouldn't go back. I begged him to let me take his spot. We all look alike to you guys, so no one questioned it."

I swirled the water around in my cup. When I had made up a list of things I had to worry about, identity theft had not been on the list.

Perhaps Horton took my silence as displeasure because he raced on to defend himself. "I've always loved computers and machines and all that. I knew more than enough to take his spot. He was at the bottom of his class. And I know I did a better job than he ever could have. You're happy with the work I've done, right?"

I nodded. "Of course. But why didn't you just go as yourself? You could have had a much better position on a better ship." I gestured at Eugene. "You could have gone into the private sector and studied robotics."

"You don't understand what it's like on a lava farm. The first nestling gets to inherit the family resources or maybe go off-planet, if they survive the first few years. Mostly, everyone is eaten by birds."

I grimaced. "Yikes."

"All the future litters are blacktails. We work to harness the energy of the volcanoes on the farm or mine the materials. Most of us are lost to explosions or landslides."

"Blacktails?" I obviously didn't know enough about

Ignesians.

"Our tails get all charred. It's a nasty nickname they give to those that are good for nothing more than manual labor."

"Oh, Horton, that's pretty lousy. I'm glad you didn't get killed on the farm."

"Are you mad at me, Captain?" His eyes were dark and shiny, and the corners of his mouth pulled down. He never demonstrated much emotion, or at least I had struggled to detect it when he did.

"It's not the most convenient time to find this out, but frankly, it doesn't even make the top five on my list of things I am worried about right now." I nodded at him firmly.

He let out a long sigh and patted the top of Eugene's box. "Eugene thought you would understand, but I wasn't so sure. Why don't you go sleep for a bit?"

I tried to fight the urge to yawn, but the mention of sleep brought it on like a compulsion. "I'm fine."

"No, go. You are the brains of this whole operation, and you need rest. I have Genie to keep me awake."

I went over and lay down on a mat at the back of the cave, positioning myself so I could see the entrance of the cave. I hadn't acknowledged Pox directly but had seen the creature dancing behind me as I settled onto my makeshift bed. I put my own water next to the mat and a small cup next to it. I lay down and sneaked a look at the rear of the cave. Pox was curling up on the bottom corner of the mat, his back to me.

I never decided to close my eyes and fall asleep, but it happened anyway. In my dreams, I found myself fighting James again. Sometimes, it was the night we broke up, my heavy black eye makeup rolling down my face as I cried, then in the next instance, I was older and on my ship, explaining that I hadn't murdered anyone.

The scenes were seamlessly meshed together, the emotions the same. In each, I couldn't understand why

James didn't believe me. But I also held back some of what I knew because I didn't want to trust him. I was reliving the same experience over and over, but this time, I might not lose just my fiancé. I could lose my life and freedom.

Something pulled me from the dream, and despite the dream feeling like it had lasted an eternity, I also felt that I had done no more than blink. The entrance of the cave was pitch-black and the fire low. Horton was slumped down, his large head resting on the wooden box containing Eugene.

I didn't know why I woke until I heard a faint whine and the soft pitter-patter of tiny feet on the mat behind my head. I slowly rolled over and saw Pox pacing next to me.

My momentary pleasure that he had gotten so close to me melted into confusion at his quiet distress. Everything was then clarified horribly when I saw the thing crawling down from the hole in the back of the cave. The spider was the size of a car.

CHAPTER TWENTY-ONE

I blinked repeatedly in some misguided attempt to dismiss the image. The spider wasn't moving very quickly as it crawled down the wall, but even as I watched, another leg poked out of the hole. It was no wonder the cave had been so empty. It was the entrance to some underground vortex of mutant spiders.

My brain was unwilling to accept that the spider was as large as my eyes showed me it was. Perhaps it was just really, really close to me. I sat up slowly, locking my two eyeballs on the spider's eight black orbs. It was dark in the cave, but enough light shone from the fire that I could see two curved pincers on either side of its mouth. They twitched like it was eager to eat me.

I put one hand in front of Pox, shoving him behind me, as with my other hand, I reached back to grab the gulper tooth. "Horton, Eugene? A little help."

I brought the tooth in front of me, gripping it so hard with both hands that the edge bit into my palm. The spider hit the ground, pincers quivering in the air as though trying to catch a scent.

"Raph! Chloe!" I attempted to throw my voice to give them warning as two more spiders exited the hole and started to descend the wall.

Pox let out a few noises that sounded like a dog's bark crossed with a cat's yowl. The first spider seemed to smile in satisfaction. The pincers on either side of its maw were slick and shiny. The smell set my throat aflame. I coughed and crawled backward.

Until then, everything had been moving slowly. Every photon of light hitting my eye burned itself into my memory with crystal clarity. But suddenly, it flipped, and everything happened at once.

Raph shouted, "Crap on a cracker!"

Chloe screamed in one long high-pitched screech.

The spider moved toward me, grabbing at me with one of its legs. Pox raced between us, barking and snapping at the spider. In a movement as fast as lightning, the spider grabbed Pox instead of me. The little animal let out a scream of terror and pain. I snapped into action. I whipped my arms out, wielding the gulper tooth like a sword.

But I had no experience with swords. I'd never used anything bigger than a kitchen knife. But the suppressed rage of the past few days gave my arms a strength and speed that they might have been lacking on a more relaxed week. Roaring with anger, I swung the tooth hard at the thick black appendage that had snatched Pox off the ground and was bringing him to the spider's gaping maw.

I had thrown my whole body behind the swing, expecting resistance, but the green bone sliced through the spider's leg like a hot knife through oatmeal. The spider screamed and pulled back, bumping into the two spiders behind it. I grabbed Pox and swept him into my arms. His tiny toes gripped me along every bit of skin they could reach.

Horton caught me by the shirt. "We have to go!"

Chloe's and Raph's receding figures were racing toward the exit. The spider I had fought was still quivering near the back wall, but a new wave of spiders had started to move forward.

Horton opened his mouth and let out a long deep roar that sent such a visceral sense of fear through my body that I had already run a dozen strides before I realized I was moving. Pox was still screaming in alarm as he crawled up my body to grip my neck with his paws. A wave of spiders pulled apart our mats as they flooded across the cave.

Horton passed me. "Run faster!" he shouted.

I tore off after him as the *tappity* noises of the spiders and their chittering sounds filled the cave. We burst out onto the red sand. Twin full moons hung overhead, filling the beach with silver light. I ran to catch up with Raph and Chloe down by the shoreline.

"They won't leave the cave," said Horton.

The interior of the cave was black, and it took a moment for my eyes to register that it was caused by the mass of spiders rather than a lack of light. I could catch flashes of light from our fire and the occasional item being thrown into the air.

"Now we know why such a 'nice' cave was empty."

Raph rubbed his hands up and down his arms before giving in to a full-body shiver like a wet dog. "Spiders! Why did it have to be gross, hairy—ugh! Chloe, why didn't you tell us they were so big?"

Chloe swallowed. Her eyes were wide, and her gills quivered. "I had no idea. They said the spiders were as big as a horse, but I don't know how big a horse is, and they exaggerate all the time!" She was on the verge of hysteria.

I stepped between them. "In this case, they weren't exaggerating. Do you know—"

Pox lost his grip on my neck.

I reached up, and he whimpered under my touch as I pulled him into my arms. In the moonlight, I could see a dark-red patch on his belly and blood oozing from a gash on his side. He let out a pained squeak before his eyes rolled back in his head, and he became a dead weight.

CHAPTER TWENTY-TWO

"Pox?"

Chloe caught my arm. "The spider venom! Did it touch him?"

My throat was practically welded shut with fear. Perhaps it was that Pox had raced to save me or, even more likely, this was the final snowflake that shifted my entire hillside into an unstoppable avalanche. From the murder, to the accusations, to an engine fire that had nearly killed one of my crew members, then to my own kidnapping, then to being swallowed by a gulper, and to surviving a giant spider attack, it'd been a bad day. Pox dying was the one thing that might push me over the edge.

I took a deep breath and dropped the tooth I still had clenched in my other hand. "Do we have any supplies?" I moved to a slight depression where water had been trapped as the ocean receded, and I lowered Pox's body into the chilly liquid.

He trembled as the saltwater soaked his fur and turned the little pool red with his blood, but his eyes didn't open. I continued to wash him, but the red jelly-like patch stuck to his skin seemed to grow in front of my eyes. After touching the warm, sticky mass, my fingertips started to tingle, and I swallowed hard, wondering what I had just exposed myself to.

I patted my clothes, but only my mother's Bible was there. Taking it as a sign, I murmured a quick prayer for a miracle then turned to see if the others had something more physical to offer.

Chloe felt around on her clothes. "I still have these in my pockets." She pulled out the bar of soap and the vitamin-C skincare product.

Raph leaned over to look. "You brought beauty supplies?"

I grabbed the soap from her hand, tore off the paper covering, and ran the bar over Pox's fur. The gelatinous mess attached to the fur started to disengage, and the heat and tingling in my fingers lessened. "Do you know anything about the venom? Anything at all?"

"Eugene, see what you can find out." Horton kneeled next to me, cupping his large hands together and scooping up water to pour over Pox.

The little wooden box flashed its light, indicating deep thought.

Chloe took the bar of soap from me and held it as I worked the suds into the caline's fur. "Um, not a lot. It's dangerous, but some of the Ceruleans make a drink from it. It's super-duper dangerous. It's both venomous and poisonous. It's this icky green-brown color until they add something to it that makes it edible."

"What do they add? It must neutralize it."

Pox stirred in my arms, twisting around to look up at me. He panted heavily and whimpered. He still had an oozing wound on his side, and small blisters were forming on the delicate pink skin underneath his fur.

"I don't remember. That show was a bunch of seasons ago. It's like a yellow fruit and sour. They had little slices of it, and they squeezed it into the tea made with the venom. They reenacted a traditional meal including the tea. One family on the planet controls the supply, and it is only good for a few days. You can only have one drink. I just don't remember anything else."

A small dot of hope started to burn in my chest. "Was it a lemon? Does that sound familiar?"

"I... I don't know," she wailed.

"Correct, Captain Laika." Eugene interjected. "The information that I can access says that ascorbic acid, which is vitamin C, can be used to neutralize the venom. This is most commonly done by squeezing the juice of a citrus fruit into the venom tea. This could be the juice from an orange, lemon, grapefruit—"

"Thanks, Genie." I grabbed the bottle of vitamin-C skin serum from Chloe and used my free hand and teeth to unscrew the top. I poured a generous amount onto Pox. "It's okay, baby. This will help," I cooed even as a part of me acknowledged that I was practically hysterical. I tried to sniff back my tears.

"Come on, little buddy," Raph said, leaning over my shoulder. "You're part of the team, just like Genie over there."

The tension around Pox's eyes eased, and he stopped whimpering. His breathing slowed to a deep and steady pace. I continued to work the goo into his fur, and my fingers no longer tingled and burned.

I sniffled again then broke into a cough, casting a glance back to the cave. It would be just our luck if the spiders swarmed from the cave while I was distracted. I was shaky and weak. I couldn't even imagine how many hours it had been since I had deep, pain-free sleep for a full shift. I yawned. I was running out of resources and strength. "Horton, how long was I asleep?"

Eugene responded. "It was seventy-three standardized minutes from the time that you last spoke until you called for assistance."

My yawn was spreading around the group. Chloe opened her mouth and gills wide. Raph copied her, his white teeth glowing in the dark. Horton followed suit with his head flipping back like a puppet and exposing row upon row of sharp teeth.

"I am all out of ideas and options," I admitted. I was feeling sick from my injuries and the continual pumping of adrenaline into my system. I was finding it difficult to regulate my body heat, and I sweated and shivered at the same time. "Chloe, do you know anything that might be useful?"

Raph muttered under his breath. "She'll remember once we are about to die."

"Hey!" she shouted at him. "It's a show mostly about dinner parties, throwing drinks in each other's faces, and gossiping. This other stuff is just casually mentioned here and there."

Raph jabbed a finger at her. "Okay. Then besides the metal-eating sea monsters, spiders that want to eat us, and cute little pets, do you know anything about the planet? Anything useful?"

She threw her hands in the air. "They don't care about lying, but being a bad host is the worst. They dress outlandishly and wear too much makeup, and that includes the men. They distrust the fleet. They will give you anything, but then again, they are rich, so it doesn't really matter. They could talk for a million years about who did what to whom, and the perfect apology makes up for anything. Is any of that useful?"

I sighed. "Not at this exact moment." But then I started to think about our situation. "What about the justice system? Someone is trying to kill us. Would that be their version of the government or military? Or could that be someone acting without permission?"

"Oh!" She pulled her head back in surprise. "That is a good point. If they had started a nasty rumor about your husband's pool, then I would believe a civilian did this. But since someone is trying to kill us, it must be with the authority of the king. No civilians have that kind of weaponry, or any at all. It's all banned."

"Good," I said, rubbing the last of the ascorbic acid into Pox's fur. The angry red flush of his skin was relaxing into a slightly upset pink. I pulled him against my stomach and wrapped the bottom of my shirt around his body. "What is the king like?"

"According to the cast, he is handsome, though he isn't my type."

"I was thinking more about his personality. Is he just? Fair? The kind that flies off into a murderous rage and attacks fleet officers for no reason?"

"No, not really. I think he is mostly hands-off when it comes to day-to-day stuff, but he is the final word on any matter. A few seasons back, Octavia accused Balenciaga— those are two of the House Mavens—of cheating her in a land deal, and somehow, they were able to take the matter in front of the king to decide. His word is final. He tries to be fair, though I got the feeling that he was swayed a lot by flattery and what sounded best rather than the law."

Pox shivered and moved in closer, tucking a nose under his back foot then letting out a big sigh. I stroked his back, and he shifted to press against my palm. "How did they get a meeting with him?"

"I don't know. You guys are really overestimating the educational value of this show. I swear I'm not holding back anything."

Raph looked ready to come back with some comment, but something caught his eye. He pointed toward the cliff.

My breath caught in my throat. On a trail down the cliff and halfway across the beach were at least three dozen people, many of which were carrying torches. A shuttle appeared, cresting the cliff.

CHAPTER TWENTY-THREE

My brain spun in circles. I hoped to assemble a plan, but nothing was coming together. None of us had shoes, let alone enough supplies to survive for more than a day. But I wasn't going to give up, even if it didn't seem possible that we could outrun even those people, let alone the second shuttle that had just appeared overhead.

But then another part of my brain started to notice details. The people approaching us weren't marching in formation or holding weapons. They were talking loudly and laughing. The men wore colorful suits, and the women had on long dresses that trailed in the sand. Many of those not carrying torches were holding their shoes in one hand and drinks in the other. They didn't even appear to notice us much beyond a few quick waves as they moved toward the shore.

Overhead, the shuttle paused and fired a shot.

I ducked down at the sound, but the shot went straight out over the ocean then erupted into a burst of blue light that exploded like a flower before dancing down to the water. A second and third shot replicated the process with a green firework then an especially impressive white one that filled the sky.

The ocean churned as gulpers rose to the surface. I stepped back on instinct, though they had to be a kilometer out from the shore.

Chloe was staring at the group of people moving across the shore. "Don't be mad at me. There is literally no way I could have known this."

"Known what? What in the universe is going on?" I asked as I turned to Raph and Horton, who shook their heads. Even Eugene somehow managed to look blanker than normal.

A woman spotted us and waved. "Chloe! Darling!" She broke into a trot, headed straight for us.

She appeared very similar to Chloe. Her gills were quite visible because of the sparkly glitter brushed on to accentuate them. Her makeup was expertly done. Even in the dark, the colors were bright enough to glow. Her hair was a bright orange that I had not seen naturally occur in citizens of her planet.

"Hello, Mother." Chloe stepped toward the woman and extended her arms for a hug.

Raph's mouth dropped open. "You have got to be kidding me."

The two women hugged and exchanged air kisses before Chloe tried to step back.

Her mother caught her around the shoulders and turned her face to the light. "You are so thin, my dear. And I don't understand why you and your…" She looked us over carefully before picking a word. "Um… your *friends* are down here? Why didn't you come to the house? Or better yet, why didn't you just tell me that you were coming? I would have sent one of Auntie Messi's vehicles to pick you up. But really, dear, you should have told me that you and guests would be here. It is rude to show up without an RSVP."

"Mother," Chloe dragged out each syllable into a full sentence, "I know that."

"Well, clearly you don't since you didn't tell me that

you were planning on joining us at the wedding. Your auntie will be thrilled that you are here, obviously, but she is going to need to make up extra rooms for everyone and make your little green Ignesian friend a comfortable setup." She turned to Horton. "Dear, what can we do to make you most comfortable?"

"Wait, wait, wait." I finally got my voice back, and my brain was reasonably caught up. "Chloe, you have an aunt on Cerulea, and you didn't tell us?"

"I didn't know. Last I heard, Aunt Messi stilled lived on Aquaria. It's not like she's my real aunt."

Her mother gasped. "How can you say that? She loves you just like she was blood and has been such a dear friend of mine for years, just *years*. And I told you she bought a home here when I sent you the invite last month."

Chloe folded her arms across her chest. "Did you send it electronically?"

"You can't send a wedding invitation electronically. People will think you are cheap. And it was just so lovely. Heavy paper from real trees, gold lettering. And they had a professional calligraphy artist hand-address each one." She clasped her hands to her chest.

"I've told you before that any physical mail takes at least eight months to be delivered."

"I wrote on the outside that it was very important. Surely, your little fleet could handle just a small task without screwing it up."

"Mother!" An orange blush crept up Chloe's face, and her gills twitched. She waved a hand at me. "This is my captain, Elizabeth Laika."

Chloe's mother narrowed her eyes at her daughter before turning a dazzling smile on me. "You will need to excuse Chloe for not properly introducing us. I am Madam Persephone Darrian , first child and eldest daughter of the House of Roses, holder of the scepter, and guardian of the rising seed and sun." She extended her right hand, palm down.

Diplomacy was an area that was as comfortable as breathing, though it had been a long time since I had used my formal introduction. The last time was when I was a witness at my uncle's trial, where I had been vilified and humiliated.

"I am Elizabeth Laika, the last of the Laika, first travelers of intraspace, captain of—" I stopped abruptly, realizing that I wasn't the captain of anything anymore. My ship was nothing more than dust in the outer atmosphere of a hostile planet. "It is an honor to meet you, Madam Persephone Darrian. Chloe is one of the best crew members that I have been blessed to work with."

Madam Darrian quirked an eyebrow and cut her eyes briefly to her daughter before looking back at me. "You may call me Persephone." She directed her statement to the group but didn't bother to continue with the introductions.

The fireworks had been providing a shifting light palette to the mother-daughter reunion. The underlying tension built similar to the explosions overhead. It felt like a timer counting down to an explosion.

Persephone snapped open a fan, and we all jumped, even Pox, who peeked out of my shirt to sniff the air. "Where is your luggage? I do hope you remembered to bring your auntie a hostess gift, especially since you forgot to—"

"I did not forget anything. I've told you that I can't run off to every wedding, party, or graduation you invite me to. I didn't even get the invitation. This was an emergency. Someone is trying to frame Liz for murder!" Chloe yelled at her mother.

I stepped a little closer. "Easy, Chloe."

She blushed a little and lowered her voice. "We're in danger. Our ship blew up a few hours ago. How did you *not* know that? Didn't you see the explosion on the horizon? Our shuttle exploding?"

"Well, isn't that just terrible?" Persephone said as

though Chloe had just admitted to misplacing her favorite bracelet. "You know, I think I heard about that. The gentleman next to me mentioned something about it at dinner during the cheese course. Cheese is an Earth delicacy. It is so delightful, but don't ask how they make it. So primitive."

"And you weren't in the least bit scared for your oldest daughter?"

"Of course, I would have been petrified with fear if I had known. This is exactly why I told you that you shouldn't join the foolish fliers."

Chloe's face slowly transformed from anger to frustration then embarrassment. "Don't call the fleet that. We have gone over this a million times. It is an honorable career, and one I excel at."

"It's a good career for those who don't have better options." Persephone looked at me quickly as though she had just remembered that I was there. "I am sure you and your crew are all very talented," she said, waving one hand, "but Chloe had all the best growing up and a future ahead of her"—she cut her eyes back to her daughter—"as soon as she gives up her job at the flying circus and comes home."

Chloe was muttering and sputtering, but tears were also sneaking out of the corners of her eyes. "Mother…"

I stepped forward, positioning myself between them just enough to draw attention to me. "Persephone, now that you have learned of our tragedies, I am sure you can imagine what a hard day we've had. We haven't had a really good sleep in quite a few days."

"But you can't miss the rest of the show. After the fireworks are done, they feed the gulpers out in the ocean. They save up all the scrap metal they import from recycling services then shoot it out over the water on the double full moon. It is quite a sight, seeing them breach the surface and snap up anything and everything."

"I think we've seen enough gulpers for several

lifetimes." I made a large show of yawning then rubbing my back as though it had never ached so badly in my life. They said the best acting was rooted in truth, and the truth was my everything hurt.

Persephone grabbed my arm then turned me back toward the cliff. "Let me show you to a set of rooms in the guest wing. The bedrooms are just stunning."

I saw a lit-up building at the cliff's edge and some people mingling to watch the fireworks. I patted her hand, which rested in the crook of my arm. "I have no doubt that you will be the most gracious hostess we have ever had the honor of staying with."

As we walked, she smiled and twisted slightly to speak to Chloe trailing behind us. "You didn't tell me how delightful your captain was. But don't worry. We can talk all about it tomorrow." Her voice held a tone that sent a shiver down my spine.

Chloe sniffled.

CHAPTER TWENTY-FOUR

The next morning, I woke up wheezing in panic, which had become my habit over the past few days. But this time, I wasn't being attacked by spiders or recovering from passing out or being kidnapped. I was in a bed with really soft sheets in a cool room where fans moved the air.

My body still ached all over. When I started to move from my side onto my back, I realized there was a furry weight pressed against my upper back. Adjusting my position made Pox let out a pathetic little squeak. He rolled over, exposing his belly and twisting his head to stare at me with one open eye.

The venom wound already looked much better than it had the previous night. One of the guests was an animal doctor and had been able to give the proper treatment, though she said that what we had already done on the beach had probably saved Pox's life.

Pox had been changed by the incident. Though he was still hesitant around everyone else, he had declared me to be safe and sane. He stuck close to me while I cleaned up in the bathroom and insisted on perching on my shoulder while the doctor had looked us over. We were beat up and worn out, but safe for the moment.

I rolled out of bed and flinched when my feet hit the cold flooring of some hard substance, possibly natural given the erratic red patterns and the way the floor smoothly transitioned to the same material of the wall and ceiling. I could feel the heat being drawn from my body as I tiptoed across the room. I stumbled and fell to my knees when Pox raced between my feet.

Up close, I recognized the texture as being similar to the flooring of the cave, and combined with the fact we had gone downstairs to reach the bedrooms, I was pretty sure my room had been carved out of the cliff itself. That wasn't surprising.

I took care of business then splashed water on my face before examining it in the mirror. The pain and drama of the past few days seemed to be etched into my face. The wrinkles around my eyes seemed deeper, my cheeks were hollower, and deep smudges lay under my eyes.

I shuffled back into the bedroom. I knew that my crew members had been given rooms in this wing. Persephone had used false names to introduce us, except with our host who knew the truth and swore she would tell no one. There had even been a guard placed at the entrance to our wing.

I lay back on the bed, breathing deeply. I would go check on everyone in a few minutes, but first, I needed to meditate and pray. I wanted to be at my best so we could come up with a plan.

When I woke up again, I had no idea how long it had been. This time, I felt fully awake, and my mind was clear. I revisited the bathroom then searched around for my clothes. I had slept in a traditional Cerualean night shirt that skimmed my knees because someone had taken my clothes while I was in the showering suite at the end of the hallway. Apparently, no one had returned them, so I had to go out in the Cerulean outfit.

Pox was balanced on my shoulder and licking at my ear, but it was too much strain on my injured neck, so I put him on the floor. He barked at my ankles then bounded down the hall ahead of me when I exited my room.

At the end of the hall was an open area I had passed through last night. It had chairs and couches that were now occupied by my crew. Plates of food were spread all around. My stomach growled at the sight of them. Unlike the strictly controlled ship food, this meal smelled of yeast, cheese, and sugar.

I didn't wait to ask for permission. I grabbed a still-warm roll from a plate and bit through the hard crust to the soft interior. I chewed a few times then swallowed long before I was ready. The food felt like it was slicing open my throat, but I pressed on by picking up and sipping a large glass of mystery juice that tasted sweet and foreign.

I drank down half the glass while giving nods to everyone present, which included Chloe, her mother Persephone, Horton, Eugene, and Raph.

Pox crawled up my body by jumping and grabbing the edge of my sleep shirt, then he dug his claws into the material to pull himself onto my shoulder, where he wrapped his tail around my neck. He extended his long snout toward the bit of bread, whimpering and quivering.

Up close, I could see that his black nose faded to a delicate pink in the middle and glistened. I knew it was cold and wet from waking up to it resting on the back of my neck. I held the hunk of bread closer, and Pox bit off a huge chunk then settled down on my shoulder. He munched away, causing a sprinkling of crumbs to fall down my neckline.

"Oh, Chloe, why don't you eat like your captain? She will plump in no time and look like a real woman," Persephone said as she wrapped a pastry sprinkled with dark shiny glaze in a napkin and passed it to her daughter.

Chloe's shoulders rolled forward, and she hung her head low as she grabbed the pink-and-blue roll. She stuffed it into her mouth with more anger than hunger.

I ate a bit more as I tried to get a read on the room. No one was in danger that I could see, but there was a silence that felt stifling. The only one who didn't seem to be avoiding eye contact or awkwardly eating was Persephone, who sipped her tea.

I finished off my drink and put down the glass. The others were also still in the night shirts we had been provided, except Horton and Eugene, as neither wore clothes at the best of times.

"Persephone, could you please check on our clothing?" I asked sweetly. "I would like to be appropriately attired so that we can thank our host properly."

She looked at me, startled, and for a second, I thought she might pass the task off to someone else. But I had carefully chosen the wording of the request so she would want to comply.

"Don't slouch, Chloe," she snipped at her daughter before putting down her tea and coming over to place a hand on my shoulder that didn't have Pox on it. "You're such a gracious guest. I will return soon." She flowed out of the room, the draped material of her dress fluttering behind her.

I grabbed a cut-up fruit and popped a few pieces in my mouth. "This tastes like garlic and orange. That's super weird." I sat next to Chloe. "Let's huddle up and make a plan."

She nodded and bit into her pastry. She pulled a face then put it down and turned to me. She opened her mouth to talk, sighed, and closed it again.

Pox crawled down my arm, which involved a lot more pinching than I liked. He put one foot on Chloe's knee to extend his head and grab the abandoned pastry.

Chloe squealed when she was able to run a hand over his body before he pulled back to eat his stolen goody in my lap. "He let me touch him. He's so soft." She sat up a bit taller.

Horton, with Eugene in his lap, pulled over a chair, as

did Raph.

I didn't feel quite as captainly as normal, given my lack of pants, but it wasn't the time to waffle. We hadn't been alone since Pox's injury. "Eugene, did you download that information from the work units in the cave?"

Eugene's red light flashed. "Yes, but it was an assortment of information from travel brochures, official statements, and current news organizations. Would you like me to repeat it all?

"No, but please fact-check what I have put together. Last night was the double full moon which is why they were shooting off fireworks at the beach."

"Correct. That occurred around the primary landmass of Cerulea in about a dozen locations, most of which are near towns larger than this one. Ninety percent of the population lives within ten kilometers of the coastline, five percent live at the castle, working for the king. The castle is located in the center. The remaining five percent live in transient locations, such as—"

"Thank you, Eugene," I interrupted. "That means that over the next two days, the king will hear cases and rule on them. Correct?"

He blinked. "Yes."

"Then by fleet law, if the king rules on my case, they have to consider that evidence before charging me. From experience, if he rules that someone else is responsible for the murder, it is very unlikely that they would go against that evidence. And since I *am* innocent and the evidence is just circumstantial, I think they would accept the king's ruling."

Raph sucked air through his teeth. "Can't we just get off this planet? I don't like this."

"I'm not crazy about it, either, but all the major hubs of transportation will be monitored as well as our monetary accounts. And right now, I trust an unknown king more than fleet police. If James and Officer Girlfriend catch me first, they're likely to exact their own justice."

Chloe patted my knee. "You must have been a really lousy fiancée." She said it with more than a bit of awe.

I didn't have time to correct her. "Eugene, I know that the future princess will be taking a train to the castle. Apparently, anyone can take it. Has that already left?"

Eugene's light flashed as he processed the question. "The train leaves from the depot in four standardized hours. That depot is in the nearest large town, located ten kilometers away. It is between a large retail location and the nearest shuttle launch location. A brochure says that most of the attendees of the wedding will not be taking the train because it arrives two days prior to the wedding. Mostly, it will be filled with people too poor to take a nicer commercial shuttle or skip."

"What's a skip?" Chloe asked.

"It is similar to a shuttle but cannot leave the atmosphere. They are much cheaper," I answered. "I was thinking that maybe I should go alone to the king to plead my case, then—"

Everyone was shaking their heads, but Raph was the first to speak. "No, Cap. Not going to work. At least not for me. We go together."

I blew out a sigh. "We need a way to alter our appearance in case we run into Vanessa, Wylene, Rick, or Todd."

Chloe scrunched up her nose. "Who?"

"Vanessa is going to marry the king. Wylene is her younger sister. Rick and Todd were the two men."

Eugene piped up. "From my records, Rick was registered as the Cerulean ambassador, and Todd is his valet."

Raph grabbed a roll and bit into it. "If they're on the train, then why don't we just corner them and demand they admit that they killed that dude and framed you? Or at least interrogate them?"

"No, no one is doing anything. I'll plead my case to the king at a public trial. It's a risk, but it seems like the best chance I have." I looked everyone in the eye to make sure they understood how serious I was.

Chloe tipped her head. "How do we know they won't just kill us when we reach the castle?"

Eugene's light flashed for attention. "Once on the castle grounds during the time of the king's deliberation, every person and creature is treated as innocent until they speak to the king."

Raph didn't seem convinced. "And if the king is behind the murder and wants you to take the fall?"

"It's a gamble but at least a public one. At the least, I will be able to plead my case in front of an audience." I didn't want to discuss all the things that could go wrong, so I stood up. "So it's been decided. When Chloe's mother returns, we will dress and thank our host. I will request—"

Just then, Persephone wafted into the room. Several people entered behind her, carrying large bundles of clothing.

She clapped twice and waited dramatically. "Once you all are dressed and thank our host, I am taking you off-planet, back to my home on Aquaria."

CHAPTER TWENTY-FIVE

I stood up and plastered a fake smile on my face. "Persephone, that is so kind of you, but we can't leave the planet."

"Pish posh. I've already made all the arrangements. The shuttle will be ready in about two hours. Since it is privately owned, no one will be looking too closely. Chloe's father is already calling the best lawyers to represent all of you. It is the perfect solution."

I eyed her suspiciously. "Flight manifests have to be public when a shuttle plans to leave the planet's surface, according to intraspace travel regulations."

She gave me a wicked smile. "Not if you have an A2B license for low atmosphere travel. You don't need a manifest, and once we're airborne, should we just happen to change our minds..."

"That is not what the regulation is intended for."

She laughed and turned to the rest of the group. "Your captain certainly does know her rules." She looked back at me. "Honey, it's called a loophole, and they are intended so people like me aren't stuck in the bureaucracy meant for the poor. Oh, don't scowl like that. This is by far the best solution. You all will be safe and protected someplace comfortable while this whole sordid mess is fixed."

I sat back in my seat. She was right. My own issues were only part of the problem. My crew had saved me at risk to their lives. Even if we got out with our lives intact, their careers were at risk. Eugene wasn't supposed to exist. Horton was impersonating a sibling. They all had stolen a police shuttle after defying direct orders from the fleet. How had things gotten so crazy? "Persephone, I'm not sure we can trust any shuttle pilot to be discreet enough. Surely, they have all been warned about us."

She gasped. "Of course we can trust Jones! He has worked with the family for years now. He would never risk his job over some petty fleet squabble."

Raph eyed Chloe before turning to Persephone. "Wait. You have your own shuttle?"

"Obviously. Between Chloe's father's work and my very active social life, it only makes sense. We used to just charter, but it became so inconvenient and they made such a big deal if you were an hour or two late. If you would like to sit in the cockpit, you are welcome to do so. Maybe you could even fly a bit. We have an emergency kit, so we can remove the braces from your arms. Surely, they are healed up by now, and you'll be able to take the shuttle for a spin."

"No. I'm sure they are just—"

"It's the newest model. It has heated seat-warmers and those fancy glasses for intraspace entry."

He perked up. "The ones that let you see the dimensions shift? Maybe I *will* check it out." He turned to me. "If the captain decides we should do it."

Chloe was eating with an intensity that seemed more about hiding her face than anything else. I had always noticed that she seemed a bit spoiled and out of touch, but I was learning exactly why she might be that way. A family that owned a shuttle was really beyond any standard of riches I was familiar with. Even with my family's money, before it had been stripped by the government during the trials, I was nowhere in the ballpark of that kind of old-planet wealth.

Leaving the planet was a risk for me, but staying was a bigger risk for my crew. It was a decision I didn't want to make, but it was the right one. "Thank you, Persephone. I think you are right. We'll go with you."

She nodded as though she had never doubted that was the case. "I brought you suitable travel clothing. Even a smock for you, dear." She patted Horton's arm. "We must hurry, as I want you fed and dressed within the hour so you can thank your host adequately. Then we must get on the road. Chloe, why don't I help you get ready? I can tell you all about Harvey. He is looking for a bride, and I already rang his mother to see about throwing a little welcome-home party for you two to get to know each other again."

CHAPTER TWENTY-SIX

The next few hours were a whirlwind of excitement even by my new catastrophe-affected standards. A lot of that was because Persephone never left my side and talked the whole time. She already had the next several months of my life mapped out.

She followed me into my room with the clothing she expected me to wear. "It will look so lovely on your figure. I know you are on the slender side, but some men really do like that. Choe's father works with so many rich men from off-planet, I am positive that one of them would just love to marry you and settle down." She shoved the dress at me and pushed me into the bathroom to change, though she put a foot in the door when I tried to close it.

"Thank you, Persephone, but I do love my job." I had only been with her for about ten minutes, and already, my head felt like it was in a vise.

"Of course you do, but there are other things you could do, like start your own delivery service or even a high-end charter business. Be your own boss. That's where the real money is. Of course, you would need to stay on Aquaria, but we would take good care of you, all of you, even your little lizard friend."

I could see that nothing was going to slow her down as she continued to drone on about the tax rate on Aquaria and a never-ending list of her neighbor's son's roommate's dad, who worked for some government agency, and all the ways they would help me.

I tuned her out as I slid into the dress, which was tight in the bodice then flared out into a large skirt made up of many layers of semi-sheer lighter-than-air fabric. Every movement I made, no matter how subtle, sent the skirt fluttering to life

With Persephone's prattling in the background about the colors I could use to brand whatever company she had settled on my running, it was like an eerie score to a dream I'd slipped into without realizing it. I could start over, fresh and new, and maybe even shed the last name of Laika, which had been passed down for generations since two of my relatives, a married couple countless generations back, had been given the right to pick their name when they were the first pilots to transverse intraspace, an act that freed all creatures in the universe from the confines of lightspeed travel.

They had chosen Laika in honor of those who had sacrificed their lives for science by choice or through mechanism of a government bent on advancement. Their trip had been doomed from the beginning as an experiment, their new names etched on their tombstones and their parents given money in compensation for their inevitable deaths.

It was a surprise to everyone when they not only lived but were able to return to Earth, changed in a way no one understood. They never felt comfortable on Earth again, just like every generation after them all the way to me. I was the last living member to hold the Laika name. Planet life made me twitchy. The time I spent on Earth for training was something to be endured, and though I was happy to vacation on other planets, the stars were always calling.

My parents had described it as an invisible cord was always drawing them back. Back then, it made no sense to me because I lived on a spaceship, and it was like trying to describe water to a fish. It was only when I left that I understood. I used to sneak out at night to sit under the stars, gasping for air like a fish on the beach.

When I had finally gotten off-planet and back into space after my training, when the war was over, I had cried for hours. The relief was immeasurable but so was the grief. I was an orphan by that point, and I would never navigate the stars with my parents again. I hadn't really felt their loss until we had slipped into intraspace and, for the first time in my life, my parents hadn't been at the helm.

Whatever easy out Persephone was offering me wasn't something I could consider, no matter how prettily she painted my future life. I grabbed my Bible off the counter where I'd left it next to the Gulper tooth and tucked it and the tooth away in the dress. My gown was beautiful and had deep pockets, all I could ask for in formal wear.

"Well?" she shouted through the crack in the door.

I stepped out. "Yes?"

"Did you hear anything I said?" She reached up and adjusted the strap the smallest bit.

"Persephone, I really appreciate all the advice but..." I hesitated, trying to figure out how to state that I had no intention of staying on Aquaria before she started planning business meetings. I decided to go for something that was still true, even if it wasn't my prime motivation. "I could never start a business because of my past. You probably don't know this, but I was on trial for—"

"No one cares about that. Not only were you found innocent, but"—she leaned in—"next time, you will be more careful."

I contained my gasp and stuffed down my protests that I hadn't done a thing. It was not the time to get on a moral high horse. "Of course. I should have known you would want to know all about me once your daughter was assigned to my ship."

"It was more than that. Her father had you investigated before we had Chloe assigned to your ship."

A cold, prickly sensation went down my neck. "No one knows who they will be assigned to beforehand."

Pox, perhaps sensing my emotions, tucked his head under my skirt and pressed against my ankles as if hugging me.

She fluffed my skirt one last time and stepped back. "You know that things are different when you have money. We wanted Chloe to enjoy her time away but not too much, so she would be back home within a few years. Her father pulled some strings to get her assigned to the most boring ship we could find. We investigated you to make sure that you wouldn't get her into trouble. That didn't work out as we had hoped, obviously, but the experiment is over. Chloe will come home now and live out her life just as I planned."

CHAPTER TWENTY-SEVEN

The next few hours were a blur as I heard that phrase over and over again in my head. "Live out her life just as I planned." My stomach twisted and turned, and a clammy sweat broke out on my upper lip that had nothing to do with the oppressive heat outside.

I knew I was barely present through the job of greeting and thanking our host and loading up the vehicle, but no one really noticed. And Persephone was busy directing a bevy of servants. Somehow, we were packed and leaving despite my inability to fully connect with reality. My brain was rolled inside me. I crunched the facts, trying for another plan and running through my options. We were all safe for the moment. No creatures were trying to kill us. Not fire. Not guns. But still, I felt the tightening grip of anxiety that we were headed down the wrong path.

Due to the overwhelming amount of luggage Persephone had brought, we couldn't ride in one car. Instead, Persephone, Chloe, Horton, and Eugene rode in one of our hostess's large vehicles, while Raph and I squeezed into a smaller one along with the rest of the luggage.

Our vehicle was driven by Persephone's personal

shuttle pilot. Apparently, he had to pull whatever duty the family asked of him. The vehicle was a car-hovercraft hybrid and would slide into the shuttle, meaning it had only the barest of features. It was slower as it cruised a few feet over the sand and turned corners rougher, but Jones, as he'd introduced himself, handled it well.

I was glad for his company. He and Raph hit it off instantly since they'd gotten their flight training in the same area of the east coast of North America back on Earth. They started discussing the town then transitioned to what life was like on Aquaria and all the best places to eat.

Raph sat in a chair next to Jones, but after a handful of glances back at me, he excused himself from the conversation and unlocked the chair to spin it around to face me. I was still mostly lost in my thoughts, staring out the window and stroking Pox, who had easily settled in life as a lap pet.

"Cap, you okay?"

"I can't shake the uneasy feeling that we are on the wrong path."

"Then let's change the plan," he said.

I tore my eyes away from the landscape, which was red on red on top of more red. "Don't you want to know why? Tell me that I am overreacting? Ask at least one question before we throw a workable plan out the window?" I couldn't hide the stress in my voice, though perhaps letting it show was something I did on purpose. It had been a long week, and I needed to have an honest opinion.

Raph studied my face. "Do you know why I was so quick to agree that we change the plan?"

I thought it was a hypothetical question, but when he waited for my reply, I let out a sigh. "No, I really don't."

"Let me take a different angle. Do you know why we came to rescue you, even though those officers said that you hadn't been kidnapped but had escaped on your own?"

"Wait. They said that?"

"Focus. We came after you because we trusted you wouldn't have left without letting us know. We knew you were innocent and didn't need to escape. Because we are a team, and we take care of our team. The way we saved Horton from the fire and the..." He looked away and seemed to be debating with himself whether he wanted to finish the sentence or not.

"Saving Horton was a bit different. He was going to die."

"And so would you have without our help."

I opened my mouth then shut it only to nod in agreement.

He continued. "You're not the only one around here with a sense of honor. You are a good captain and person and don't deserve to die being framed for someone else's dirty work. Plus, we *wanted* to because we like you. And I owe you."

"Owe me for what?"

"I don't want to dig up old news, but I think you need to know. When I first got to the ship, it was my last stop. If I could have gotten through two more months of service, I could leave at the five-year mark and go back to Earth. I knew that it would take at least four months for you to discharge me, so I had no reason to even try."

I was quiet and tried to give him space to work through what he wanted to say. I had seen his record when he joined my crew and had been able to guess how he would be feeling, but I had no idea the extent that it had impacted him. I had been pretty wrapped up in my own hurts and issues to notice.

"I was pretty tough on you, Cap, pushing boundaries and stuff. The other captains I served under over the years had always made a point of letting me know how little they respected me, my abilities, and my opinions. I figured you would be the same, so I didn't really give you a chance. Then you sat me down and told me how it would be. I never really apologized for my attitude during that time."

I smiled a little. "You saved my life several times this week, so I think we're even."

He let out a bark of laughter. "Fair enough. It really meant a lot to me when you told me that you believed in me and that you would give me the freedom to be me. And you told me that you thought I had the potential to be the best navigator in the fleet."

I wasn't sure I had said all that, though I would now. Maybe I had been in such a haze of depression that I had said it and didn't remember, or perhaps he had heard what he needed in the subtext. "I noticed that you seemed happier after we talked."

"It was more than the talk. You walked the walk as well. You listened when I made suggestions and didn't hassle me if I cut loose in the evenings. Then when we got our first bonus, you split it with the crew. Suddenly, navigating was fun again. Horton and Chloe feel the same. We have freedom and a job we love. Plus, the money isn't bad. And you are a big reason for that."

I felt guilty. I had pictured the past two years as my own personal hell like a spoiled child because I didn't get a shiny new ship headed out on the best job. I had missed what was around me. How much had I missed by sulking in my room? "Thank you, Raph."

"So now that you know why I trust you, will you tell me why you are feeling uneasy?"

The vehicle had moved into a highway where traffic was controlled and directed by lines and lights. We were now traveling on wheels that sent the vibrations of the road transmitting through my body.

"Chloe's mom bribed the fleet to get Chloe put onto our ship. She doesn't intend for Chloe to leave again. It doesn't seem healthy. I know we are supposed to respect other cultures, but did you see how Chloe looked this morning?"

"Like a whipped dog with its tail between its legs?" he

asked.

Pox raised his head to whine gently.

"Shh. Not a real whipped dog." I scratched behind Pox's ears until he settled down. "I know it is the safest plan, but at what price?"

"We could still do the train idea. I even know how to use all the makeup to disguise us." He jerked his head back toward Jones.

A staticky voice rose from the dashboard. It was too far away for me to understand the words, but when the transmission was done, Jones maneuvered the car to the side of the traffic and turned to explain to us. "The other car was pulled over. I'm going to take a different way. Persephone said to take good care of you guys."

He slowed to a stop and pulled up a map on his console.

There was a hiss of a door opening, and my safety restraints unlatched automatically. A hand reached in and pulled me out of the vehicle.

CHAPTER TWENTY-EIGHT

I had let my guard down, which was a big mistake. I was on the ground and away from the vehicle before I could even start fighting. Officer Girlfriend had the advantage, and she dragged me to her car. She was hitting me with something that made all of my muscles contract then give out. It was like all of my limbs were trying to head in a different direction of their own volition.

Whatever she was hitting me with made it so I couldn't get in a clean hit, though I did manage to do something to her knee before she shoved me into the backseat. Snot was running down my face, and one eye kept twitching. But with my good eye, I was able to spot Raph and Pox running toward us as we pulled away.

I thought to try to open the door, but the handle was gone. It hadn't been removed in the smooth way of a law enforcement vehicle. This handle had been ripped out, leaving behind a bevy of loose wires that gave me a shock when I touched them. There was a clear divider between the driver's seat and the rest of the automobile, and the faded signs in the back indicated that it was meant to be some kind of car for hire for tourists coming in on commercial shuttles.

My vision was clearing as much as it could, given that I was sliding around on the plastic seat as Heather took each corner on two wheels. Because it was an old-fashioned car without hover capabilities, she was forced to stay on the streets.

The way she was moving set off alarm bells, though they had already been ringing from the fact that she had zapped me half to death and kidnapped me. I'd been kidnapped twice in two days. I wondered if that was a record.

There was a variety of vehicles on the road, from cars like we were in to hovercars and cycles. But she was treating the others like bumperpods from traveling carnivals, clipping them as she aggressively passed.

"What are you doing?" I asked when I had control of my voice again. Gathering information was vital to my survival.

"Oh, wouldn't you like to know?" she spit back at me. Her voice had an edge of hysteria and bitterness that indicated she was on the verge of losing it.

"Where's your boyfriend?"

She slammed her hand on the steering wheel so hard, I wasn't surprised when it cracked. She roared, "I'm saving him by getting rid of you. You have ruined his life. His career! We can't be out in public together, and we're so much in love. He can't have the job he should because of you!"

Having found the sore spot, I poked a little more. "Won't put a ring on it, eh? Maybe you just aren't his type."

She roared again and completely twisted around to face me, pulling on the steering wheel in the process. "You've been a stain on our life together, but no more. You are going to get what you deserve. Those Ceruleans swore they would take care of you, but I should have taken care of it myself. Just like they asked me to at headquarters."

We ran roughly into the side of another vehicle, and

she turned back to handle the driving.

I swallowed hard. "Who? Who set me up?"

"Shut up! We had a whole plan, and this murder worked into it perfectly. Those two Ceruleans were more than happy to trade dirty work. Take care of two asteroids with one rocket, so to speak. But then your crew wouldn't listen to me!" She slammed her hand on the broken steering wheel, and when she pulled it back, blood was rolling down her wrist.

If she got me into the desert, who knew what she'd do to me? I looked around at the vehicle, hoping that maybe I could signal for help. Most of the other vehicles had pulled back, wary of an old-fashioned car careening and banging into everything that moved or stood still. But there was one I recognized as a small creature leaped from dashboard to driver to passenger then back again.

I blinked back tears, relieved that Raph and Jones were coming for me, even as I wasn't surprised. Raph had said we were a team, and I believed him. I slid back into the seat and buckled up with a thin strap across my waist, hardly advanced safety features. I wasn't sure what might happen next, so I kept my hand hovering over the release latch.

"Getting rid of me won't fix everything," I said.

Heather growled and turned to face me. "You've ruined every—"

Jones maneuvered up to the driver's side and rammed the car. The impact spun the car around and over several times. Heather screamed as we rolled. Air bags were exploding, and all I could see were flashes of sky then pavement. When we finally stopped moving, I was hanging upside down. I undid the safety strap and collapsed onto the ceiling of the car.

Officer Heather's purple hair was visible in the darkened car, and she let out a groan as I crawled out. I dragged myself across the pavement, cutting my hands on shattered safety glass. Trying to get up, I stepped on the hem of the dress and ripped off the bottom layer.

I had just managed to get to my feet when I was hit hard in the center of my chest by a small but insistent ball of fur. My face, neck, and ear were assaulted by licks, and tiny paws scratched at whatever skin was exposed.

"Easy, Pox." I scooped him up to my chest, though his tongue continued licking anything of mine he could reach.

I attempted to walk only to discover that my right ankle no longer wanted to hold my weight without screaming pain. I sat back down on the ground just as Raph reached me. He took my elbow and pulled me up.

"My ankle!" I yelped, hopping and stumbling along next to him.

"Sorry, Cap!" he shouted. He picked me up and flung me over his shoulder. His clavicle bit into my stomach, and Pox banged against his back. I grunted, and Pox barked in time with each jogged step.

Raph threw me in through an open doorway, and the world spun around me as Pox continued his job of licking every square inch of my face. My ankle yelped with pain, while a growing ache moved across my hips and up to the shoulder I had landed on, which had also taken the majority of the impact from the air bag.

My brain felt like scrambled eggs, and my right eyelid twitched. But it could have been a lot worse. Raph got into his seat as I pushed up to a kneeling position.

Jones was at the steering wheel, staring at the car I had been in. It was flipped on its roof and leaking fluids. His eyes were unnaturally wide, and his skin was ashen. He muttered, "She can't just take you. It's not right. You can't just grab people like that." He turned to me, and when he gestured, his hand shook uncontrollably. "I said I would take care of you."

"And you did, Jones. You saved my life." I grabbed his hand and found it as cold as death. I pulled him back beside me. "Raph, you need to drive."

There was an unnatural metal-on-pavement screeching,

and the car listed like a wounded animal. Raph shifted to hover mode and backed up. The front fender fell off with a crash.

Jones caught my hand. "Go to the train station like you said earlier. I know someone who can get you a ticket."

I nodded, and from the corner of my eye, I saw Heather crawling from the wreckage, her eyes wild and crazy. She raised something from her hip, a black square, and pointed it at the car.

"Go!" I shouted, thumping on the back of Raph's chair.

CHAPTER TWENTY-NINE

I swayed back and forth with the rhythm of the train and inspected my image in the mirror of the private bathroom at the rear of the last car. I tried to imagine seeing myself with fresh eyes. Would I be recognizable?

"Can't we just hide in the bathroom until we arrive?" I asked Raph.

In answer to my question, there was a furtive knock on the door. "Let me in."

Raph unlocked the door and opened it.

A train employee stuck his head through the doorway. "You have five more minutes max. They are about done checking all the tickets, then everyone will be able to move around. They were fully sold out, so I couldn't get you a seat."

I gritted my teeth. "I thought anyone could ride the train?"

"Yes, it's free, but people still reserve tickets because seating is limited. I got you onboard, but that is all I can do. I need to unlock this bathroom soon, or my boss will ask questions." He started to squeeze back out of the door then paused. "You aren't going to cause any trouble, are you?"

I shook my head. "No, we just want to lie low and get to the king for a fair hearing."

The blue skin between his eyebrows scrunched up. "You don't need to hide to do that. You would have immunity."

"The fleet doesn't think so."

He grumbled a string of syllables that I didn't recognize beyond having the cadence of a traditional curse. "The fleet is nothing but a bunch of sanctimonious busybodies."

"Wait. If we don't have a seat, then where can we go?" I asked.

"There are two cars in the middle of the train where people can mingle. One is a bar. Everything but alcohol is free. The other is an observation car. You can hang out in one of those until we get to the station at the castle in a few hours. I have to go, but you better be gone when I get back in"—he checked his watch—"three and a half minutes." He slammed the door behind him.

I sighed and looked at my reflection again. "I guess this is a good enough disguise if we don't run into anyone."

Raph tutted. "Are you questioning my abilities? You look nothing like yourself. I used contouring to hide your features, and the bright eyeshadow changes the shape of your eyes. Combined with the outfit, no one should know you."

I looked down at the gorgeous dress that he had shredded with a small pair of scissors he had found in Persephone's makeup bag, which we had "borrowed" when we left the car, promising Jones that we would be careful.

The skirt was short and stuck out in every direction, but more noticeable were the strips of fabric he had used to wrap my injured ankle then twisted around each calf. He called the wraps "leg warmers," as if I needed to stay warm, given the temperature outside and inside the train.

Pox was asleep at my feet. I hadn't even given him a thought until we were halfway to the train and he was still bounding alongside me. I worried he would draw attention until I noticed a few others with the same creatures in tow.

I turned to Raph and flinched when I caught sight of his face, which had matching pink-and-yellow glittery eyeshadow, making his eyes look as though they were framed by two flowers. "Geez. That catches me off guard every time I look at you."

"Exactly."

"But isn't the point to blend in? Everyone is going to be staring at us."

He pulled his head back. "Did you notice the people on the platform? There were a ton of people done up like this. They call it Valley Girl style after some old-fashioned fad on Earth."

I rolled my eyes. The history that Earth preserved was strange. They lost a bunch of science, but thank goodness, they saved old fashion magazines. Somewhere in there was some telling psychology about what people really valued. "And how do you know what it's called?"

"I started watching some of those shows I get for Chloe. We had a lot of hours to kill on the ship, especially since Horton and Eugene had things running so well."

"Did you know about Eugene?"

"Nope, but it all makes sense now. Don't tell Chloe about the shows." Raph grinned at me. "I like giving her a hard time."

"Like you did when you said she wasn't paying attention? Why didn't you know any of that stuff about the gulpers and spiders?"

He shrugged. "I wasn't in the best mood when I snapped at her, and I've only watched about six episodes, half of which just showed the people at a party. Come on. We need to get out of here."

"And the fact that we aren't Cerulean isn't going to give it away?"

"They have a high tourist population and enough immigrants, many of which dress in the Valley Girl style.

Plus, with Pox on your shoulder, we'll fit right in. Now, we need to get out of here. Remember to roll your shoulder forward and slouch. You're not a fleet captain right now. You're a disillusioned outsider."

"Not much of a stretch," I grumbled as I stepped out of the bathroom and pivoted around a line of people waiting to get in.

As I made my way to the cars the employee had mentioned, I had to admit that the disguise seemed to work. The population on the train was half Cerulean, but the other half was a mix of off-world visitors, and sure enough, a good portion were dressed like us and with similar makeup.

As we passed, we got suspicious looks and clutched belongings from the Ceruleans and casual nods of acknowledgement from the other Valley Girls, whether male or female. But no one seemed to recognize us or call for fleet backup.

I kept my head ducked as the other biggest risk was running into the particular Ceruleans who had been on our ship and must have had a hand in the murder, something I intended to prove to the king to clear my own name. When we finally got to the drink car, we grabbed two beverages and moved to a small two-person table in the corner.

The atmosphere was party-like, and no one was giving us a second glance. After thirty minutes, the press of the crowd caused a stifling heat. But no one had even looked in our direction the whole time, so I started to relax. Since neither of us wanted to get up, we were carefully nursing our drinks a sip at a time.

"Raph, how do you know how to do makeup?"

"I went to an arts high school on Clara before I joined the fleet. The acting majors were always putting on plays, and none of them wanted to be the waitress or boyfriend or whatever small parts were needed, so those of us in other majors would fill in. It was a low-pressure way to hang out and meet girls."

"If you weren't an actor, then what did you study?"

"Music. You should come hear me play sometime when we get a new ship."

"Totally," I said as I gazed out the window. There might not ever be another ship. "Why did you join the fleet?"

"Music is a tough career, and I thought I wanted something predictable. I love navigating, but the environment doesn't really match my personality, until I worked with you. You get my artist ways."

I nodded. "I can see you being a musician."

I looked away from the window as two Cerulean men squeezed in at a table directly behind Raph. They were practically shouting at each other over the noise, and the sound carried well to where I was wedged in the corner.

I grabbed Raph's hand and leaned in to whisper, "Don't move. Right behind you is Rick, the ambassador, and Todd, the valet."

He frowned. "Who?"

"The two Ceruleans from the ship."

CHAPTER THIRTY

To say that Rick and Todd were behind Raph would be overstating the fact. As more and more people pressed into the space, they had backed up until the table and chairs were crammed into half the space that they should have been.

Rick, the smaller of the two men, had his chair next to Raph, and he sat shoulder to shoulder with him, though he faced the opposite direction.

Todd adjusted his seat, banging into Raph. He partially twisted around and said, "Sorry."

Raph grunted back a general "No worries" but kept his eyes on me.

I kept my head down, staring at my drink. Raph had combed a large section of my thick hair in side-swept bangs that I could use to hide most of my face.

Ambassador Todd leaned over and jabbed a finger at Rick as he spoke. I struggled to hear what they were saying. The rowdy crowd around me only let me catch bits and scraps.

"Mind your own business. You don't know anything about—"

Rick reeled back. "I don't understand! Why do you

have all that?"

Todd sneered and bit out some words that were lost in his clenched teeth. He caught my eye briefly then leaned closer to Rick. "If you tell anyone, they won't believe you. But I have an offer. After the wedding, I will get you a good station off-planet. Great pay for your whole family. You have three little ones, right? It will be nice and safe for them."

A chill went down my spine, then Todd looked up and stared at me for two beats too long. I could barely see him in my peripheral vision. He didn't seem to recognize me unless he was an excellent actor, which I couldn't put past a career politician.

I made a big show of finishing off my drink and shaking it at Raph. I mouthed, "Wait a few minutes," and he nodded in agreement.

I resisted the urge to bolt from my seat, instead trying to embody the petulant, angsty energy of a youth angry with the world. I definitely had a handle on the anger part. I had done everything right, and yet my life had spiraled out of control and landed in the dirt. But even as I pushed through the crowd on a train that carried me ever closer to my fate, my brain wouldn't allow me to lie to myself. I had lost a lot, but I had pulled through. Even with unknown forces stacking the deck against me in the trial, I had been found innocent.

And my reward? On one hand, I could say it was the worst job in the fleet, and I had been saying just that since I got the posting. But was it fair? I had been able to sock away money every trip to get me back to financial solvency, something I had lost during the trial.

Day by day, I had found people that respected me as a captain. That wasn't a given for any captain, let alone one with a checkered past like mine. And it was more than chance. Chloe's family had bribed someone to place her with me. Raph was being punished. Horton had sneaked onboard using his brother's name.

None of us should have been together, but we were and had saved each other's lives. It was almost like someone had a greater plan. I paused briefly to say a prayer of thanks and pat the Bible still tucked in my pocket with the gulper tooth. I had gotten this far, and in that moment, I believed with my very soul that I was going to survive this. *But how?*

"Is that your boyfriend?" a voice purred into my ear.

It took me a second to register that the young Cerulean with bright-teal eyeshadow that extended across fifty percent of her face was addressing me. I twisted back to point at Raph. "Him? No, just a friend."

A second Cerulean wearing a black lace fingerless glove slithered up to me and gave him a wave. "I bet he has a huge pool."

"What?" I pulled a face. "He doesn't have a pool. Not even a house."

They both gasped and stepped back.

The first one shook her head. "Uh, okay. That's weird."

Raph came up to join me just as they disappeared into the crowd. "What was that about? They looked interested."

"That's what I thought, then they asked if you had a pool and left when I said no." I tried to push through the crowd and head toward the other car. I wanted to get as far from Rick and Todd as I could.

Raph hissed in my ear, "You told them that I didn't *have* a pool? Do you know what that means?"

I was trained in diplomacy and should have known better than to answer a strange question without double-checking local terminology, but I had a good excuse for being off my game. I shoved my way between two large groups and found a bit of open space on the other side to step next to Raph. "They weren't literally asking about a pool, were they?"

"It's a slang term for manliness, like being strong and a protector and such. I don't know all the implications, but saying I didn't have a pool was like saying that I am a bad man or unmanly. Basically, it's an insult." He scrunched his eyebrows together at the reflection on his reputation.

"Got it. Say no more. Let's go—" I stopped and grabbed Raph's arm to spin him around.

I had gotten a good look into the observation car, and I saw Officer Heather entering. I checked the entrance of the bar, and my heart sank to my feet when I spotted James at the door. He was moving in our direction.

We were surrounded.

CHAPTER THIRTY-ONE

I backed away and wedged myself between two Ceruleans at the bar. I pulled Raph in close so our faces were inches apart, our frantic energy bouncing off each other. Both cars were very crowded, and it would be difficult to move through the people, but that would only buy us a handful of minutes.

I cast my eyes to every corner of the train. Maybe once James moved past us, we could double back and exit the car. But stationed at the entrance was a new threat, an officer in a fleet uniform. Their backup had arrived. Our game of cat and mouse was no longer so simple.

Raph followed my sight line and nodded, instantly taking in the information. "Perhaps we could—"

My attention was dragged off him when the drunk female Cerulean next to me grabbed my arm and shouted into my ear, "Do you think people can change?"

I spun around and shouted at her face, "Seriously!" I was about to be squashed like a bug, and someone wanted to have a heart-to-heart chat?

"My sister is getting married to the man I love, and she's a terrible person. She once tried to poison me because I spilled ink on her favorite dress. I think she's

163

done worse." The woman squinted at me. "Do I know you?"

"You've *got* to be kidding me," I mumbled.

Officer Girlfriend was halfway through her car. James was making slower but steady progress through the car.

"You have to help me." She shook my arm. "I don't know what to do."

"I am the last person to ask." I stared deeply into her eyes, searching for any clue to my own survival. "You have to tell someone… everyone. Lives depend on it."

I twisted out of her grip, and without consulting Raph, I shoved Pox into his arms. They were both safer without me, especially where I was heading.

I pressed through the crowd, aiming for the space between the cars. When we moved through the train earlier, I had noted that the space between train cars was open to the air. I had seen enough classic movies to know I could climb onto the roof of the train, though most of those movies ended badly.

But my feet were moving on instinct, fear and adrenaline taking over my higher brain functions. I was out the door of the beverage car and halfway up the ladder attached to the side of the car before I even realized what I was doing.

Sheer momentum carried me up to the top. I started crawling across the roof. The train was barreling toward the castle. It was exactly like the few remaining stone structures back on Earth, even down to the moat around the outside. The track was headed straight toward the large structure, then it curved to the right to go around the moat where a station was visible a few kilometers past the castle.

The train was moving at a fast enough speed that the wind was roaring in my ears. When the engine shifted and brakes squealed, I gripped a ridge so hard that my knuckles turned white. I was out of my depth. If I slipped over the side, I would hopefully die quickly from the impact or from being dragged under and cut in half by the steel behemoth.

I should have surrendered. I should have taken my chances that they wouldn't shoot me on sight on a crowded train. This was not how everything was supposed to end. Maybe it was the wind or how close I was to the end of my life and my hope, but tears streaked down my face, and I didn't even attempt to wipe them away. When James stuck his head over the edge of the car with his ban trained in my direction, his expression was filled with pity.

I huddled on the roof like a rat. I was at the end of my options, short of taking my own life. Even if I could unhook my hands, I knew I couldn't go that way. Generations of Laikas had headed into certain death and survived. I would fight until the choice was taken from me.

"Liz!"

"No!" I screamed back.

He started to crawl toward me, his face tight as he inched closer. "Why are you doing this?" he bit off as he closed the gap. "I know you are innocent."

I gasped, and my fingers slightly loosened. I adjusted my grip on the ridge. It was a trick. He was trying to get me to lower my guard. I doubled my resolve to escape when Heather slithered up behind him.

The train was slowing down. She rose onto the balls of her feet and started inching toward me. She had dried blood on her face, and her makeup was smeared, giving her a wild, frightening appearance that matched the craziness in her expression. We locked eyes, and hers radiated pure hatred and uncontrolled malice.

She accomplished in me what the train hadn't. I was able to move. I unlocked my hands. They shook uncontrollably, but I inched backward, the hair on the back of my neck rising like that of a feral animal.

"Stand down!" James shouted at her. Something crossed his face. *Annoyance?*

I scooted farther away from them. If I could reach the castle, I would surely be safe, but was there any way to escape them? I felt like a deer being pulled under by a pack of lions. It was the awareness of the end that made it so terrible. It would have been a mercy to have died in the engine fire. Why had I been brought through so much just to fail in the end?

Something snapped inside me, and all the pity and fear coalesced into anger. I felt pure hot rage for the man I had loved and trusted, who had not only left me but was abusing his power to destroy me.

"How could you?" I screamed.

"Me?" He glared at me. "You are the one who ran away."

"Saying it doesn't make it true. You and your girlfriend framing me shows that you have no morals."

I was heaving huge breaths, barely able to hold it together, but I could still tell that something was off. James stared at me blankly. The look that passed over his face was pure confusion.

Heather looked between us, realizing the same thing. "Shoot her! Then we can be together."

The pieces came together for James before my eyes, and I realized what I had missed all along. He had never said they were together. She was the only one who had said that, and he had never been present for her declarations of love. He had always been a rule follower, and it was unlikely that he had changed that much in the few years since I had known him.

He pulled away from her. His attention was split between us as he realized the real threat.

The smallest glimmer of hope rose in my chest, like the sun peeking over the horizon. "She said they sent her to get rid of me. She gave her ban to the Ceruleans and had them abduct me, but I got away. Where's her ban? When she grabbed me earlier, she would have used it if she still had it. She would shoot me now. And who unlocked the doors of the ship? How could the Ceruleans and I have escaped at all unless someone with security clearance had unlocked them?"

"No, she wouldn't." But his voice lacked conviction. His whole belief system was crumbling around him, but he still moved on instinct.

He hadn't changed, and maybe I hadn't either. "Tell him the truth!" I screamed.

Heather reached out and latched on to his wrist. "They said we could be together, that she's the only thing holding you back. They said that if I got rid of her, if I pinned this murder on her somehow, we could be together as partners, and you would love me. We might never get another chance."

He recoiled from her. It was clear what he thought of the proposition.

She saw it as well. Whatever she believed, perhaps what they had convinced her of, all crumbled around her. Maybe it was the fact that she had too many witnesses to get away with it or the fact that he would never love her that broke her, but we would never know.

She stood up, and the wind caught her body. In slow motion, she was swept off the train, which was on the long bend just before the moat. She never reacted. She appeared as calm as if she were falling into a pool of warm water. Her body disappeared on the inside bend of the curve.

The tears I had been holding back poured out. I couldn't even process the meaning of everything that had come out, but my body reacted instantly to the emptiness in her eyes as she disappeared from sight. It would haunt me forever.

I would have stayed there in shock even as the train whistle pierced the air and the brakes locked in response to the accident, but James crossed the distance between us. He grabbed my shoulders and shook me hard. I realized that he had been shouting at me.

"You have to go! I don't know who I can trust. Go!" He gestured toward the castle.

I pushed away from him. Before I could second-guess him, I took two quick steps and launched myself off the moving train, heading toward the opaque water of the moat. I hit the surface like a ton of bricks, and everything went black.

CHAPTER THIRTY-TWO

I walked into the castle yard, sopping wet and missing one shoe. Rather than ditching the single kitten heel, I walked with an uneven gait. I appreciated even the minimal protection from the rough gravel.

Stomp. *Squelch.* Stomp. *Squelch.* I crossed the empty yard and entered the enormous door to the castle.

Inside were dozens of people lined up around the perimeter of the main room. They sat in mismatched chairs from rough wooden benches to ornate, embroidered armchairs. Heads all around the room looked up to watch me wobble across the floor. I stopped and pulled off my heel. I then left wet footprints the rest of the way.

I approached a female Cerulean sitting at a large table. She was filing her pale-blue white-tipped fingernails.

She didn't bother to look up as she slid a clipboard toward me. "Fill out this form. We should be able to fit you in tomorrow. What crime are you here for?"

I grabbed the clipboard and a pen. "Murder."

She dropped the nail file. "What?"

"I didn't kill anyone, but I am being framed for murder," I clarified.

She narrowed her eyes. "There hasn't been an unsolved murder on Cerulea for decades and decades."

"Technically, it happened in space. I'm a fleet officer, and there was a murder on my ship. One of the officers—"

"Oh my gosh! I know just what you are talking about. The king will be so excited." A dark-blue tint rose in her face even as her feet danced beneath the desk. "I mean, this is all terribly sad, but... please take a seat, and I will get to you in a minute. You don't need to fill that out." She snatched the clipboard from my hand and disappeared through a door. As the door closed, her voice carried out and echoed in the large chamber. "Janie! Janie! We have a hot case!"

Everyone watched me with unconcealed interest, except the Cerulean I sat next to, who promptly vacated her seat to race across the room and point over her shoulder to me.

This was it. After everything I had gone through, it came down to trial by bureaucracy. Fitting and yet sad. I dripped water onto the floor, running over my defense in my head. By the time they called my name, I would surely have the most perfect defense in the galaxy.

But instead, my name was called within a few minutes. The secretary was back and didn't even bother to close the door behind her, instead calling out to me, "Hey, murderer! You're up."

I stood up hesitantly. "Can you not call me that?"

"Of course! What name would you prefer?"

"Elizabeth Laika. Thank you." I followed her down a hallway, my bare feet slapping on the stone and water still dripping down my legs. "Can I change? Or at least clean up a little?"

"Sorry. You should have done that while you waited. Here. Sign this." She paused in front of a door and shoved a clipboard at me. "It says that you accept the king's ruling, which will be given at the end of your presentation."

I signed my name. "Then what?"

"If you are found innocent, then you can go free with a small reward for your inconvenience. If you are found guilty, then your punishment starts immediately, which for murder of a government employee is…" She flipped through a booklet then ran a finger down a page in the middle. "Death by beheading. Not too bad."

"Sure… totally."

Before I could say more, I was shoved out the door and into one of the largest rooms I had ever been in. Hundreds of Ceruleans sat in chairs dozens of rows deep, and every one of their eyes was on me as I crossed the open space to stand behind a podium that stood in front of a large chair.

In the chair was a male Cerulean dressed in ornate clothing. Even without knowing the local standards of beauty, I could guess that he was extremely attractive. It was partially the extreme confidence with which he moved. But the biggest giveaway came from the several female Ceruleans in the front row, holding signs with variations of "I love you, King!" printed on them.

I put my hands in my pockets and pulled out my damp Bible and the gulper tooth. I placed both on the podium. A soft murmur spread through the crowd at the sight of the broken tooth. I shifted my feet. It was a terrible time to give in to the fear of public speaking. I needed to focus on something else, like giving a presentation that didn't end up with my head on a platter.

I closed my eyes and sent up a quick prayer. Everything I had encountered would also be my salvation. I opened my eyes as the king started to speak.

"Elizabeth Laika, you have been accused of—" He paused to look over the paper someone handed to him. He made a small noise of interest, and when he looked at me again, it was with considerably more attention. "I was told this situation had already been handled."

I gave a little nod. It was time to pull out all my

experience in diplomacy and acting. "Yes, they have been attempting to *handle* me for several days, but I have survived. I knew that my only chance of a truly fair trial was with you."

"Why not your fleet?"

I let out a loud sigh. "Unfortunately, there are those in the fleet, much like your court, who can't be trusted."

"Why is that?"

"Jealousy."

He nodded with understanding then took a tablet from an assistant. He held up a finger, indicating I should wait while he reviewed the information. After a few minutes, he handed the tablet back to his assistant and shooed him away. "Captain Laika, a few years ago, you were on trial for financial impropriety. Is that correct?"

"Yes, but the charges were dropped due to lack of evidence."

"And the lead prosecutor is now president of fleet. I can see why you have concerns about fleet integrity."

I debated adding more information, wanting to focus on the facts, but a quick look around the audience showed them to be hanging on every word of our conversation. The people of a planet whose economy relied heavily on dramatic reality-based entertainment probably appreciated hearing all the details. Many were even pulling out an air-roasted grain to eat while listening to the case.

"The fleet sent two officers to investigate. One was my ex-fiancé, and the other was in love with him. She told me that once she got rid of me, they could be together."

The king leaned forward. "Really?"

A murmur rose in the room at the pronouncement, along with a raise in noise level that pulled my head around. James and a few other officers had entered the room and were standing at the back. People were twisting around to point and whisper. James stared straight ahead, but I was pretty sure he was embarrassed, based on the way he stood.

Then I noticed another group clustered in the opposite corner, and my heart rose at the sight of Raph, Chloe, Horton with Eugene under his arm, Persephone, and Jones. I was looking for Pox when he suddenly appeared on Raph's shoulder.

Once we locked eyes, he vaulted off Raph's shoulder and bounded through the crowd. He bounced from shoulder to head to lap and finally to the floor to race the rest of the way to the podium.

I squatted to scoop him up, a reminder of the people who had closed ranks around me to protect and save me. Pox crawled up onto my shoulder and wrapped his tail around my neck.

The crowded let out a collective "Aww." I gave them a smile, playing up to them and the moment. This was nothing like the last time I had stood in front of a judge and jury. But that had been a solemn affair with a room so quiet that one could have heard my confidence hit the floor. This was a spectacle, and frankly, I hoped that would work in my favor.

The people seemed to want to believe me, to follow along with me for whatever reason. Maybe the general negative views of the fleet I had experienced had set me up as someone to cheer for. Maybe my likable personality had won them over. I didn't know how it influenced the king, but perhaps it would help.

He pointed at Pox. "You have made a friend. Did you find him on your journeys? They are very slow to trust."

"I did, and if you allow me to explain, I can tell you how he"—I reached up and stroked his back, and he licked my face in return—"saved my life and how I saved his in return, using this." I lifted the gulper tooth from the stand and, very slowly because I didn't want the guards to rush me, imitated cutting off a spider's leg.

The crowd gasped, and talking filled the room. In the back, Ceruleans rose to their feet to get a better view.

The king stood and raised his arms. "Silence!" Once

the spectators calmed down and he had resettled on his throne, he gestured to me. "Go on. Tell your story."

So I did. I told only the facts that I had experienced since Chloe had burst into my room to announce that there had been a murder. I related all the details of my fall, finding the body, and calling for backup. I wove together James and Heather's arrival with the engine fire, the three dead housekeepers, and my own abduction.

I made sure to read the crowd as best I could and slow down or speed up to hold their attention as I described the shuttle chase, the gulper encounter, and the spider attack. Then I praised the fireworks and the beauty of the land as I finished the story with the vehicle chase, the train ride, and my final arrival at the castle.

I had no idea how long I had talked, but I managed to hold the attention of the king.

When I was done, he nodded and gestured at me. "Fascinating story, and you surely have entertained the crowd, but you did not answer who you think the real murderer is."

I gulped hard as that was the final card in my hand. I hoped that the crowd, but especially the king, would follow me as I headed into the final act of my story, the reveal.

"I know that you are a smart man and will see, as I did, the only possible solution. Your future bride, Vanessa, and the Ambassador Rick killed the Cerulean on the ship because the victim had discovered that they were running a black-market gulper-bone smuggling ring."

CHAPTER THIRTY-THREE

The king narrowed his eyes as the humor dropped from his face. He raised his hand and waited until the room calmed before speaking. "That is a serious allegation."

I had anticipated his initial disbelief. Suggesting that the two people closest to him were deceiving him was a big gamble, but it was the truth, and the truth was the only thing that could set me free. "If you will allow me to explain, King, I can show you how it all fits together. Then you can appropriately punish those who wish to work against you."

I paused a few seconds to make sure I had everyone's attention. "The first sign of trouble was the fire. While anyone could enter the engine room, only a few high-level members of the crew and the cleaning crew would have known about the screen that needed to be deactivated to prevent the failsafe from kicking in. The fire had been caused by a handful of tools being shoved through the grate. It could have killed everyone on the ship and was dangerous to the perpetrator, but even more so, it pointed to someone who didn't have that clearance or knowledge of the engine. That leaves just our cleaning crew as possible perpetrators. They were the only ones who knew enough, yet not enough, to be so dangerous."

"Were they the type to do that?"

"I don't know much about them. Cleaning crew jobs are not well-paid positions, and they tend to cycle in and out. But an even bigger indicator of their guilt is the fact that they were found dead shortly after the fire. The killer must have paid them to disable the ship right next to Cerulea, but the killer didn't want witnesses left behind. Someone mentioned that the cleaning crew had been given tea. I was also offered tea, but I dumped mine into a plant. When I was abducted, I may not have seen the person, but I did see that the plant was dead from the poison in the tea. I'm guessing the poison was also meant for me."

He nodded and spun his hand in a "go on" gesture.

I tried to speak faster, fearing that I was losing his attention. "Then came the abduction. Officer Heather Halston told me that she had been instructed to get rid of me. When the Cerulean vessel docked, she must have helped them to do it in exchange for taking me and disposing of me."

"I was told that you must have stowed away. When they saw you running, Ambassador said that you were a criminal, and my officers went to capture you." He said it without inflection. Though I hoped that on the inside, he was reevaluating the information he had been given.

"I was knocked out and woke up locked up in a bathroom where the interior handle was removed. Did you send the shuttle?"

"My fiancée said that she was scared and didn't trust the fleet."

"Did you instruct the officers to chase us toward the ocean?"

"No. Hold on." He gestured for the assistant to bring back the tablet then spent the next few minutes reviewing information before passing it back. "The chase protocol did not follow the rules, but I do not know the reason for that. Go on."

"When I was trapped in the ship, I overheard a conversation between Vanessa and her sister. Vanessa said, "It will be like Jonah." I opened the Bible. "That was a reference to the Old Testament story of Jonah, who was swallowed by a whale. She knew what was going to happen. My guess is that they left me on the ship alone, hoping that I would steal it. But when I left on another shuttle, they shifted gears."

I moved on, wanting to stick to the important details. "The gulper tooth also gave me the idea for the weapon that was used for the murder on the ship. Our security scan can miss organic materials, such as bone or wood. A gulper tooth would have been missed by our ship's weapon scan and could have easily been used to murder the victim. But since all gulper bone is processed on Cerulea, the only way that a weapon from that material could have been on our ship is if one or more of the passengers were smuggling it."

The crowd's response buoyed me. They seemed to be connecting the dots I was laying out and finding the story interesting.

I pushed on. "On Earth, there was at one point a similar system in which a majority of the world's diamonds were controlled by one company. It kept profits up through the monopoly, but people went to terrible lengths to get their own supply because the price was so high. An ambassador who travels frequently would be an ideal candidate, and a future princess would be the perfect partner. A small amount of power is dangerous in those that are corrupt."

The king seemed to struggle with his emotions, and I gave him a moment to let the facts sink in. These were Ceruleans that he had trusted. Many people would fight back, unwilling to admit their assessment was incorrect even in light of facts. My hope was that he had already seen enough.

When he seemed ready, I continued. "She tried to poison people before, which brings me to her title of Bearer of the Venom. She had passed me tea that was brown while she drank pink tea, the result of a reaction between citric acid and the tea, which also neutralizes the venom from the spider. And I know one more thing. She doesn't love you because she spoke badly of your... pools."

A gasp went around the room, and I swallowed hard. That last bit was potentially my downfall. He was a proud man, and saying his fiancée didn't love him could mean my demise, but if he already had his doubts, it might be the cincher.

He couldn't contain the anger in his eyes. "Do you have anything else to add?"

I shook my head.

The king didn't respond other than to gesture to a guard by the door. "Her testimony is done. Is anyone here witness to these events and willing to speak on her behalf?"

The crowd turned to look in every direction. Chloe, Raph, Horton, and Jones stepped forward. They were willing to collaborate my testimony as much as they could. Then I noticed another person was stepping forward.

James pushed to the front of the room. "I am Officer James, investigative lead, and I have a lot to say about Captain Elizabeth Laika."

CHAPTER THIRTY-FOUR

I was held in a back room for hours. I didn't even have Pox for company because they wanted to examine his healing skin as evidence to see if what I had told was the truth. I was brought a tray of food, which I didn't refuse, though I did skip drinking the tea.

All I had was my wet little Bible. I decided that instead of worrying, I would read. I delved into it just as I had the previous time I sat anxiously awaiting the outcome of a trial. It wasn't an experience I had ever planned to repeat, yet fate had different plans.

I eventually decided to finish the verses in Ecclesiastes that I had started days earlier. As I paced the room for the millionth time, I read out loud, the easy rhythm sinking in and giving me peace.

"A time to weep, and a time to laugh; a time to mourn, and a time to dance; A time to cast away stones, and a time to gather stones together; a time to embrace, and a time to refrain from embracing; A time to get, and a time to lose; a time to keep, and a time to cast away; A time to rend, and a time to sew; a time to keep silence, and a time to speak; A time to love, and a time to hate; a time of war, and a time of peace."

The door creaked open, and the guard from earlier stepped in. "It's time, if you're ready."

I nodded and felt exactly that, ready. Ready for my time of peace, time to love, a time to keep, a time to speak. I was ready to face my fate, whatever it was. I was scared, but each foot moved smoothly as I followed the guard back so I could stand in front of the king again. Those who had stood witness for me were sitting in the front row, even Pox, who was curled up on Chloe's lap.

"Captain Laika," the king said then waited for me to turn to him. "Your witnesses spoke well for you, but there is still a shocking lack of proof of your accusations. While the story knits together well and is quite believable, it all hinges on one fact, that you didn't kill the victim yourself. If I am to believe your story, then two Ceruleans would be guilty."

I sneaked a quick look at James, wondering what he had said, but that thought was pushed away as it sank in that no one had said enough to convince the king of my innocence. I could feel that the ruler was torn. Heavy was the head that wore the crown, and the situation had been forced on him. I wished there was something more I could say.

He sighed. "You will be given a chance to plead your case one last time, then I will need to give a verdict on the *proof* I have. But if anyone has any information that they would like to share, this is your last chance." He seemed almost hopeful as he looked around.

"Wait!" a thin mechanical voice rang out.

I turned to Eugene, who was sitting on Horton's lap. His red light flashed.

The king gestured at Horton. "Do you have more to add to your testimony?"

Horton stood and approached a table beside the podium. He put Eugene on top of it then turned him so the light faced the king. "Not me. Eugene does."

"Eugene is a…?"

The entire crowd leaned forward in their seats.

The little red light flashed, illuminating most of the table. "I'm an artificial intelligence program. I have been gathering data since I left the ship. I have information related to the case."

"I'm sorry, but computer programs cannot testify. I can't take the information into account."

"Actually, King, anyone can testify in your court as long as they are recognized as a registered sentient being by any established government in any universe. And you, as king of Cerulea, have the right to bestow citizenship, which I humbly ask you grant me. I have information that will help you, and I wish to serve." If Eugene could have bowed, he probably would have. He didn't have any such information when we had last spoke, as far as I knew, and I had my suspicions that he didn't gather anything new using the most legal of methods. But I certainly wasn't going to protest. His existence was in jeopardy as much as mine.

The king tipped his head back and studied the little wooden box. When he spoke, his words were deliberate. "The fleet has determined that AI programs should be destroyed when discovered. Too dangerous."

Heads in the audience swung around to Eugene, waiting for his reply. Horton was wringing his hands. His eyes glistened with unshed tears.

Eugene's reply was also slow in coming, but when it did, I could hear the weight of things left unsaid, the tone of knowledge only he and the king understood. "The fleet often oversteps their authority and fears what they cannot control. You are the sovereign leader here and know what is best for those who depend on you."

Everyone, myself included, watched the king for his reply. After what felt like an eternity, he said, "And what can you offer in service to my kingdom?"

"I have proof of an ongoing conspiracy against you involving Vanessa and Rick and the smuggling of gulper bones. Additionally, there is evidence—"

"And how would you have such information when even my best—when no one else has found such evidence?"

"Captain Laika became suspicious when our ship was disabled and asked a crew member to reach out to his contacts at our destination. It appears that they had created some enemies with their dealings, and their partners were waiting for them at the destination. It seems that someone tipped off the authorities. Right now, it is all very confidential, but since it affects Cerulea, I have obtained all the relevant material for you to review."

The king stood up and gestured to a guard. "Bring the box to my office. We need a conference immediately."

CHAPTER THIRTY-FIVE

Raph, Horton, Chloe, Pox, and I huddled in a small room. Whatever information Eugene had given the king in their private meeting meant that I was no longer locked up alone, but the company only slightly lessened my anxiety. I was optimistic yet scared to get my hopes up.

Persephone had left with Jones to rest after her "eventful morning," while James had disappeared. I imagined he had a lot to report in addition to handling the death of Officer Heather Halston.

A shiver went down my back. I hadn't really had time to process her accident. She'd carried her secrets to her death. Someone in the fleet was still determined to kill me, and though I had a good guess at who it might be, I still didn't understand why. I wasn't a danger to anyone, and I hadn't stirred up any trouble beyond accidentally being accused of murder.

In fact, Cerulea might do the dirty work for them, though my fear was receding. I believed in my crew, Eugene included. Whatever he had been able to dig up could be all we needed. I was quite sure that the "how" behind how he got his information involved breaking several security features and laws. But he had risked his own existence, and the fact that he might be saved through citizenship didn't negate the risk he was taking for me.

The door creaked open, and the guard gestured for us to follow him. I grabbed one more of the chocolate caramel treats and stuffed it in my mouth as I walked out behind the others. If I was about to die, I wouldn't need to worry about working off the weight. Small bonus.

When I returned to the court, there were a lot of surprises. James came to stand next to me. He gave me a tight smile. The crowd burst into cheers. But the biggest surprise was a six-foot screen that showed the fleet leadership council watching us.

The king stood to address the entire room. "After speaking to Cerulean citizen Eugene Basaltic, I am ready to give my verdict."

Horton gasped. "Eugene took my name!"

I shushed him and waited to hear my fate. The king was a true showman, dragging out the moment until I was leaning so far forward that I risked tipping over.

"I have found that Captain Elizabeth Laika is... innocent of all charges. Further investigation will be conducted until we have rooted out all those that are guilty." He turned to the screen. "I assume the fleet will agree that this is the final ruling on the matter."

I could see the muscles in the fleet president's jaw flexing and the slight narrowing of his eyes, but when he eventually spoke, it was with the same restraint and monotone he always used at official events. "Of course. And we will also search for how Officer Heather Halston was able to avoid psychological evaluations and pull off such a plan all on her own."

Always the politician, he had deftly divorced the fleet from Heather's actions, but there was no one to prove otherwise. Except...

I turned to look at James. Though unsure of what I expected, I was surprised to see the anger etched into his eyes. He had heard her confession and knew that the fleet would not be investigating. It was the reality of the situation, though I found it unsettling that he was upset by the fact while I had so readily accepted the reality of it.

Perhaps James still held his noble belief that truth would win out, while I had been discovering that life wasn't fair. But life did reward those who fought, and I was a fighter. Maybe there was still hope for the future I had once believed was mine.

I took a look around at my loyal crew and knew that what I had was better than what I had lost.

The king addressed the fleet members on the screen. "I know you have more to say to the captain, but I must finish my presentation." He turned back to me. "Captain, your work on behalf of the kingdom will be rewarded. Your entire crew will receive monetary gifts, but you will receive the greatest gift. You will be my bride."

CHAPTER THIRTY-SIX

My heart leaped into my throat, and my legs almost gave out beneath me. James managed to grab my elbow before I face-planted.

There was a low buzz of interest from the court attendees. Turning down a suitor of his power in front of such an audience could be just as dangerous a situation as trying to beat a murder charge.

I stepped forward and did my best impersonation of a ladylike curtsy. I scrambled for what to say that would address the situation adequately. "I am honored beyond words."

"It is our custom that you take the place of the fiancée you removed... unless you have reason to believe that you are unworthy, then you can recommend another." He walked toward me.

Up close, I could read his face better. Even the highest station was held to the rules and traditions of their role. I believed that was the case in the current situation because his eyes seemed to beg me to take the out he was offering. I gave him a slight nod that only he would notice, and his face relaxed.

I turned to the audience. "I would be honored to be

your wife, but I fear that I am inferior to the task. My heart belongs to the stars, to space. I would be unworthy and incapable of serving Cerulea in the way the station requires. But I do know someone who loves not only Cerulea but adores you in the way required. Wylene, Vanessa's younger sister, spoke of her great admiration of the king and his—" I swallowed hard before I basically fawned about his appearance and manliness. "His large palace and pools. I do not believe that she had any part in the deception that took place, though your investigation will better answer that question."

The crowd oohed at the news.

The king raised his eyebrows in appreciation. "I do believe that would be acceptable." He started to turn away to walk back to his throne.

"But I would ask that I could take my caline, Pox, with me when I leave. He will be a beautiful reminder of the planet that has stolen my heart and saved my life." I lowered my head in a sign of submission.

"Of course." He gave a little chuckle. "There is little I could do anyway, as a caline bonds for life. Take him with you. You are all dismissed as I have many other cases to attend to as well as speaking with my future bride."

We were led from the room and into a back hallway. We whooped and cheered as I exchanged hugs with everyone. Then I encountered James.

Everyone else excitedly talked as I stole a few moments of privacy with James off to the side. "Thank you for speaking for me."

"I had to tell the truth."

I rolled my eyes. "Just accept the darn compliment. I swear."

He ground his teeth. "I thought something was off when you referred to Heather as my girlfriend. It wasn't in character for you, and I almost asked why you did that, but I assumed you were just being jealous."

"Jealous? No, she had said she was your girlfriend. And

she looked just like I did when we dated."

He frowned. "She did?"

"How did you not notice? Purple hair is not that common."

"It is in the fleet. Have you not noticed?"

"I don't get out much." I turned to leave. I needed to focus. For the moment, my life was safe, but my career was still up in the air. I should be okay, but I wouldn't put it past the fleet to try something underhanded.

"Wait. I need to apologize."

I turned back around to face him.

"I said you hadn't changed, and I was right—"

"I thought you were going to apologize."

"I will if you just stop talking. Geez, you never let me get a word in."

I mimed locking my lips and tossing the key then crossed my arms.

He sighed. "I said you hadn't changed, and I meant that as an insult because I was mad. But it is true because you are a really good captain. A lot of people would have never recovered from the trial, but you did. Your parents would be really proud."

"Uh, thanks. We need to go talk to the fleet and get that over with." I discreetly wiped at my tears and cursed James under my breath. He knew my biggest fear was not living up to my parents' expectations. He had no right to use that information against me, even in the form of a compliment.

The sooner I could get away from him, the better. I made a beeline for the far end of the hallway, where a guard was gesturing for us to follow him.

Once I had gathered my crew around, James initiated the connection to fleet.

The rest of fleet panel was grim faced as the president talked. He spoke as though the words were hot coals that burned his mouth. "Captain Elizabeth Laika, in light of the unfortunate turn of events, we will need you to sign paperwork stating that in exchange for none of this going on your record and interfering with your future service, no future action can be taken against the fleet or spoken of publicly."

"Cutting right to the chase, I see." The words were out of my mouth before I even realized I was saying them out loud.

The president's mouth tightened.

I briefly considered apologizing but decided against it. He had witnesses, and I needed to make a stand that I was willing to play the game but not be pushed around in the process. "My crew must have the same deal. No negative marks on their records. And I want our previous mission marked as successfully completed."

"You blew up a ship full of cargo!" he barked.

I stared at the screen with my heart in my throat. "We didn't. And if you really want to go into it, I will gladly go to fleet court and plead my case publicly. All of it."

"Fine. Agreed. Officer James Markswell, have them mark the agreement, and we will have it recorded as such."

James passed around a pad for us to sign and mark with a fingerprint.

The president continued. "In accordance, we are willing to offer you, Captain Laika, a station on a new explorer vessel in the Nighthorse Galaxy to commence three days hence."

If there was any shock left in me, I would have fallen over at the offer. My dream assignment was being handed to me on a silver platter. I nodded as though I had expected it all along, and I was glad I had the chance to play my cards. "Then since my last mission was marked successful, as captain, I invoke my right to article 104B, otherwise known as Laika's Legacy."

The president's face slowly turned red, and the microphones were muted. I could tell because an excited conversation broke out at his table, but no sound was transmitted.

Behind me, Chloe asked, "What is Laika's Legacy?"

Raph answered, "Cap's parents had a rule passed that after a successful mission, a captain or senior team member could request to keep his or her crew together. Up until then, they were at the risk of being broken up after each mission."

I nodded in agreement, though I kept my face pointed toward the screen. My parents had considered it their greatest achievement, something they could do to protect what they felt was their family. The same sense of preservation for those that served under their command was what led them to leave their ship and sacrifice themselves. Their actions had won the war.

I shoved that away, focusing on taking deep, slow breaths. I would show no weakness. Not in this battle of wills.

The sound came back on, and the president had mostly retained his color. "The position you are being offered is for an existing ship where the captain had to step down. It is set to start exploration on a new planet immediately, but only that one position is available. We will make sure that your crew members will be given equally generous offers at whatever place and type of assignment that most interests them. Or..."

He adjusted in his seat before continuing. "You can invoke article 104B, but we will need to find an open ship, and we cannot guarantee that it will be a step up from your previous job. And obviously, your crew members will be welcome to find new positions if they wish. In fact, we have found dozens of open jobs that I am sure they will jump at. But it is your decision, and you must make it now."

I took a slow breath and announced my decision. I hoped I wouldn't regret it.

CHAPTER THIRTY-SEVEN

I sat by the pool in the shade, perusing the news on my tablet. I had mostly adjusted to the heat on Cerulea and had to admit that it was growing on me, especially when I had traded running for my life for "sitting by a pool, drinking and relaxing."

Pox lay on a chair next to me, making little grunting noises in his sleep. Other than his small sounds, it was achingly quiet, and I could practically hear my eyelids blink in the stillness.

There had been nothing published anywhere in the galaxy about an exploding ship, murder, or the attempted framing of a fleet captain. It had been completely and totally covered up.

Fortunately, until a fleet shuttle arrived, the king had given me use of his vacation home to rest in. The full-time staff was a nice bonus I had thoroughly enjoyed. In private, the king thanked me for my handling of the situation and for the suggestion of his new bride. He told me if I ever wanted to leave the fleet, he would be honored to have me as his employee, which was the best offer I had received in quite some time.

The events of those days had been plaguing me.

James's apology, negotiations with the king, and my final decision had crept into not only my days but into my dreams at night. I just wanted to move forward.

I checked my notifications and discovered I had a message that contained my ship manifest, which would list my crew. I still didn't know what ship I was assigned to or the exact details of our mission, but that should arrive any minute.

"Hey, guys! Get out here!" I shouted to the house behind me. "The manifest is here."

Raph came running past me and cannonballed into the water. When he surfaced, he asked, "We going to be hauling trash to the nearest star? Delivering convicts to prison? What terrible horrible job do we have this time?"

Chloe walked over and handed me a plate of food. She squeezed in next to Pox as she finished off her colorful drink. "Don't give her a hard time. She gave up the Nighthorse Galaxy so we could be together. It will be fun no matter where we go."

"It's a job, not fun," I corrected, though I couldn't deny that having them by my side was better than not.

Horton slinked past me and fell face-first into the water. He hadn't been himself since we said goodbye to Eugene. He was putting on a brave face, but we all knew he missed his friend. Horton swam lazily across the pool, his tail extended behind him.

"I don't know what we are doing just yet, and this crew list doesn't help much. Medical technician, three custodial staff, this is all pretty basic stuff except... Cerulean ambassador? Why would we—" I lost my breath when I saw the name attached to the position.

"Ambassador Eugene Basaltic reporting for duty!" a thin mechanical voice declared. From an opening in the wall around the pool rolled the wooden box. Eugene now had continuous track wheels set up on each side and two thin arms. I spotted a few other accessories, but I could only guess at their use.

"Eugene!" Horton screamed, launching himself from the water and racing across the distance.

"Careful, Tonny. I just cleaned my optical lens."

They took a few minutes to catch up in private before Horton put him down. They joined us a few minutes later, and Eugene greeted each of us in turn.

I was so happy to see him that I didn't immediately notice the flashing light on my tablet. When I did, I checked to see what I had received. Reading over the details, I couldn't help but smile. "Guys, it's here. I have our next assignment."

ABOUT THE AUTHOR

Nikki Haverstock is a writer who lives on a small ranch high in the Rocky Mountains. She has studied comedy writing at Second City and has published 13 cozy mysteries that are heavy on the humor.

Before fleeing the city, she hosted a competitive archery reality show, traveled the world to study volcanoes, taught archery and computer science at a university and worked on her family's ranch herding cattle. Nikki has more college degrees than she has sense and hopefully one day she will put one to work.

Nikki likes to write comedy pieces that focus on the everyday humor of family, friends and the absurdity of life. She tried stand up but the cattle weren't impressed.
www.NikkiHaverstock.com